awkward stuff.

awkward stuff.

a girl stuff novel

lisi harrison

G. P. PUTNAM'S SONS

G. P. PUTNAM'S SONS

An imprint of Penguin Random House LLC, New York

alloy**entertainment**

Produced by Alloy Entertainment
30 Hudson Yards, 22nd floor
New York, NY 10001

First published in the United States of America by G. P. Putnam's Sons,
an imprint of Penguin Random House LLC, 2022

Visit us online at penguinrandomhouse.com

Library of Congress Cataloging-in-Publication Data
Names: Harrison, Lisi, author.
Title: Awkward stuff. / Lisi Harrison.
Description: New York: G. P. Putnam's Sons, [2022] | Series: Girl stuff; book 3 |
Summary: Best friends Fonda, Drew, and Ruthie make a pact
to have their first kisses on the same night.
Identifiers: LCCN 2021059904 (print) | LCCN 2021059905 (ebook) |
ISBN 9781984815040 (trade paperback) | ISBN 9781984815033 (epub)
Subjects: CYAC: Friendship—Fiction. | Kissing—Fiction. | Dating (Social customs)—
Fiction. | Middle schools—Fiction. | Schools—Fiction. | LCGFT: Novels.
Classification: LCC PZ7.H2527 Aw 2022 (print) | LCC PZ7.H2527 (ebook) | DDC [Fic]—dc23
LC record available at https://lccn.loc.gov/2021059904
LC ebook record available at https://lccn.loc.gov/2021059905

Printed in the United States of America
ISBN 9781984815040

1 3 5 7 9 10 8 6 4 2

CJKB

Design by Nicole Rheingans • Text set in Freight Text Pro

✖

As some of you might have gleaned, I dedicated Crush Stuff
to my crush, Wyatt. Cute, right? Wrong. In said dedication,
I wrote, "I hope we're still together by the time this publishes.
If not, I might have to name book three Awkward Stuff."
And, well, see the title of this book?

YOU: Does this mean you and Wyatt broke up?
ME: That's so sweet of you to ask. And, no. We're still going strong.
YOU: So what gives, Lisi? You wrote—
ME: I know what I wrote. My editors and I ended up liking that
title, so we went with it.
YOU: Well, that's awkward.
ME: Sure is. No one does awkward like I do. I literally wrote
the book on it.

Enjoy!
Xoxo

chapter one.

THE LAST TIME Fonda Miller's mother made breakfast on a school day was, well, who knows?

Joan, a feminist studies professor, believed in her daughters' right to choose when it came to their bodies. Yet, on this Friday morning in November, Joan insisted they sit at the kitchen table and eat chia pudding, of all things.

Meanwhile, she was at the counter, grinding coffee beans and humming, like it was perfectly acceptable to give someone the right to choose and then not let them choose anything.

Fonda wanted to press for an explanation, but that's what older sisters were for. Winfrey was sixteen, Amelia was fourteen, and Fonda's age didn't matter. *She* didn't matter when they were around; neither would her questions.

"It's one of the three D's, isn't it, Joan?" Winfrey finally asked. The waves were epic, her friends were at the beach, and her FOMS (Fear of Missing Surf) was intensifying. She clearly wanted out.

"Three D's? I have no idea what that means." The mess of crimson curls around Joan's face bobbed as she sat.

"Death, divorce, disease," Amelia explained, pink mirrored sunglasses already on. "So, which one is it?"

"Divorce?" Joan scoffed. "I'd have to be married first, and I'll never, ever—"

Amelia gasped. "You have a *disease*?"

"No, Amelia, I don't have a disease, and I haven't died either. I'm speaking at the Freedom of Expression dinner in Los Angeles next Saturday."

"Sounds like death to me," Winfrey mumbled.

"The topic is Stand Up to Gender Bias, in case anyone was wondering."

They weren't.

"How long?" Amelia asked.

"Saturday afternoon until Sunday morning."

"You're going to stand the *entire* time?"

Fonda giggled because, come on. Amelia was a high school freshman. She should know that Standing Up meant speaking out in support of something. Not anti-chair.

Winfrey's bright expression clouded over. "Um, quick note for you, J."

Joan folded her arms across her chest, ready but not prepared for whatever Winfrey was about to ask.

"I refuse to be babysitted by Sari Poppins."

"*Babysitted* is not a word, and your nanny's name is Sari *Sullivan*."

"Joan, she's a cheery British lady who brings crafts and uses an umbrella when it's seventy-two and sunny. What do you expect?"

Joan looked at her daughters, like, *really* looked. Then she said, "You're right. It's time."

"Time?" Fonda asked, heart beating. "For what?"

Joan took a deep breath and turned to Winfrey. "You're going to be seventeen in January, and—"

"You're finally buying me a yellow MINI Cooper convertible?"

"No," Joan said.

"A yellow MINI Cooper convertible with *surf racks*?"

"A convertible with surf racks?" Fonda laughed. "How would that even work?"

"This isn't about a car," Joan said. "It's about next Saturday night."

"No way, uh-uh, I am *not* going to that lecture." Fonda took the napkin off her lap and stood.

"Where are you going?"

"I'm Standing Up for my freedom."

Amelia removed her sunglasses. "I thought you didn't have to stand."

"This has nothing to do with standing," Joan insisted. "I was thinking of letting you girls stay here alone while I'm gone."

Winfrey jumped out of her seat. "YOU'RE LEAVING ME IN CHARGE?!"

"Yesssss!" Amelia jumped up too, and the two girls enveloped Joan in a suffocating hug.

"Wow. Someone's happy to see me go." She tried to lift her arms and hug them back, but their grip was too tight.

"I'm not," Fonda peeped, because Winfrey was going to be a tyrant.

If only they had a dad who could step in and take over. But no. Their father was a mysterious sperm donor who, according to the West Coast Cryobank catalog, loved Greek mythology, med school, and his maternal grandmother.

Joan finally managed to wiggle free from her daughters' grip and told them to take their seats. "This is not a free pass for you to go wild. It's an opportunity to prove how mature and responsible you are."

"Fear not, Joanie. I'll make sure Amelia is home by nine o'clock and that Fonda is in bed by eight thirty."

"What? No!" Fonda turned to her mother. "My bedtime is ten!"

"If you have a problem, talk to me," Winfrey said. "I'm the boss now."

"No, you're not," Joan insisted. "No one is. You're

each responsible for your own actions, but you must look out for one another and work together so everything runs smoothly."

Fonda sank in her seat. Look out for each other? Work together? Ha! According to Winfrey and Amelia, *together* isn't one word. It's three. *To-get-her*. And they always did.

The only way to save herself was to leave. "I'll probably spend the night at Ruthie's, or Drew's, so—"

Thunk! A bird flew into the sliding glass door. The girls screamed.

"Oh," Joan cried. "That's the third finch this month!"

Fonda's eyes filled with tears. *Poor little guy.* She knew what it felt like to be cruising along and then *slam!* Something unexpected stops you in your tracks and knocks the wind out of you. Winfrey's new promotion to "sister in charge" being the perfect example.

Joan grabbed her dishwashing gloves and hurried outside. Once the door slid shut behind her, a devilish smile spread across Winfrey's face.

"What's more mature and responsible?" she whispered to Amelia. "Starting our party at seven or at eight?"

"Probably seven," Amelia offered.

Winfrey drained her mother's coffee mug and slammed it down on the table. "Eight it is."

"You're having a party?" Fonda whispered. "While Mom's *gone*?"

"Well, we're not going to do it while she's here."

Fonda's stomach dipped. "What if she finds out?"

"There's only one way she will, and it's currently wearing my old denim romper and thinking I won't notice."

"You think I'm going to tell?"

"No, I think you're going to invite a bunch of your friends and wear something that doesn't make you look like me two years ago."

"Wait." Fonda drew back her head. "I can go?"

Her sisters nodded.

"And invite people?"

They nodded again.

Fonda jumped to her feet so suddenly, her chair fell over. Ava G. may have thrown the first boy-girl party of seventh grade, but Fonda would be known for having the first boy-girl parent-free high school party. Her seventh-grade status would be locked and legendary. Yes, her sisters were only including her so that she wouldn't tell Joan. But a girl had to start somewhere, and this somewhere happened to be at the very top.

✖

"Happy Friday!" Nurse Beverly smiled. Her teeth looked extra white against her too-dark-for-November tan. "Congratulations on completing the first week of our PuberTea." She lifted her great-grandmother's antique china teacup, pinkie out, and took a dainty sip. "Great job, young women. Great job."

The circle of fifteen Poplar Middle School girls lifted their old-lady mugs and politely slurped the tepid berry-flavored tea. The guest teacher was doing her best to take the cringe out of health class, but the only way a lesson about "breast buds," "peach fuzz," and "natural urges" would be less cringey, if not downright funny, was if Fonda had been in class with her next-door besties. But the nesties were out of luck. Drew had been placed in the afternoon class, and Ruthie's Talented and Gifted crew had their own thing going. Thankfully,

Fonda had her boy-girl parent-free high school party to distract her from the "science of body odor" lecture. So she pretended to take notes and got to work on her guest list instead.

When Winfrey said to invite a "bunch of friends," how many did she mean, exactly? Five? Ten? Thirty? Because Fonda already had fifteen people, and that wasn't including Ruthie's TAG crew or—

"OUCHIE, MY BRA STRAP HURTS!" a boy shouted as he passed the classroom's open door. "I NEED A TAMPON!" He used one of those high-pitched girly tones, but Fonda knew exactly who it was.

No matter how hard Henry Goode tried to disguise his voice, the deep squeak that Nurse Beverly blamed on an adolescent boy's growing larynx was unmistakable. Or maybe Fonda recognized it because Henry, Owen, and Will had been hanging with the nesties ever since their field trip to Catalina Island three weeks earlier. Which explained why fourteen giggling girls were looking at Fonda as if she was partly responsible for Henry's drive-by hooting.

Cheeks burning, Fonda focused on her party list,

willing the embarrassing redness away. Clearly, every-one assumed she and Henry were a thing. But were they? Sure, the group went to Van's Pizza and Fresh & Fruity after school a few days a week. And yes, Henry and Fonda usually sat near each other and flirt-debated topics like Twizzlers versus Red Vines, thin crust versus thick, and whether dogs from different countries bark with accents. But a *thing*? Didn't people in "things" have to agree that they were a "thing"? Didn't they do things together, without the group?

Not that Fonda minded being mistaken for Henry's other half. It made her feel mature and brave, admired and respected. Like she was part of a secret society made up of experienced girls who somehow knew what was what when it came to boys. When really, the closest Fonda ever got to Henry's body was when she grabbed his leg on the Catalina Island rock-climbing wall to keep him from falling. And then they both fell.

Still, she didn't plan on correcting the giggling girls. Why not let her reputation have some fun for a change?

"Enough about bacteria and underarm protein mol-ecules," Nurse Beverly said. "It's time for AwkTalk."

Fonda winced. The most awkward thing about the nurse's talks were her titles.

"Yesterday, I asked you to submit a question you're too embarrassed to ask out loud. Now, who's ready for answers?"

The girls sat up a little taller. Fonda sank a little deeper. She had initially written *I'm ready for my period, but it hasn't come yet. How do I speed things up?* But she was afraid everyone would know who wrote it because most of the girls in her grade already had their periods. So she changed her question to: *Do you think period purses are helpful?*

Fonda hoped that Nurse Beverly would say, "Why, I've never heard of a period purse."

To which Fonda would reply, "It's a cute zipper-pouch filled with menstrual essentials."

"Menstrual essentials?"

"Yes, Nurse Beverly. Or messentials, as I like to call them. Sanitary pads, a change of underwear, ibuprofen, Reese's Pieces . . . that kind of thing." Then Fonda would reach into her backpack and wow the class with her own period purse.

Only, none of that happened. Instead, the nurse pulled an index card out of an Asics shoebox and read: "'I can't breathe when I'm kissing a boy. Should I be inhaling through my nose or my mouth? Sometimes I hold my breath, but that feels like drowning. What should I do?'" She crumpled the card and sat on the corner of her desk. "Great question, Anonymous."

Best friends Ava G. and Ava H. exchanged a low five. Of course this was *their* question. And double of course, they had already kissed boys. Apparently, everyone had, because all around Fonda, girls began whisper-swapping opinions.

"No nose," muttered Kat Evans, a peppy gymnast with an enthusiastic ponytail. "Hold your breath and take tiny fishlike gulps."

"Yes, nose," Ava R. whispered back. "Nose breath smells better than mouth breath."

Toni Sorkin, VP of the student council, said, "It's the same breath. Trust me. Noah Suture's nose air smells just as eggy as his mouth air."

Fonda sank even lower. Had all these girls *really* kissed someone before?

"If anyone wants to know what a trained professional thinks, just ask," Nurse Beverly said in that patient, not-patient way.

No one did. For starters, no one wanted to picture Nurse Beverly kissing. For enders, she probably hadn't kissed anyone since the 1900s, and everything was different now.

They did, however, look to Fonda, who they assumed had something valuable to add. After all, she and Henry were a thing, right? They'd already kissed, right?

Wrong.

They'd never even hung out alone. And Fonda had no idea how to kiss-breathe, but she certainly wasn't going to admit that. Instead, she lifted a silencing finger to her lips like a girl who didn't kiss and tell.

Nurse Beverly began offering some gross advice about falling into a rhythm with one's partner and breathing together. Fonda immediately thought of Henry and how hard they laughed when they fell from that rock-climbing wall. How they rolled around on the mat in hysterics and gasped for air at the exact same time. So, technically, they had the rhythmic breathing thing down. Which meant they'd probably be good at kissing too. Which also meant they could try it and then weigh in on the nose-versus-mouth debate for real. But did Henry even want to kiss her? And if so, how would she know? They could start by having the talk, but then what? Who would make the first move? Once they started, how would they know when to stop? What if Fonda forgot to breathe and she suffocated? She couldn't breathe just thinking about it.

Not only was she behind on her period, but she was also behind on kissing.

Something had to be done.

chapter two.

FRIDAY AFTERNOON. OVERCAST. Ruthie Goldman's bedroom. Snacking on dried fruit. Elton John spinning on the old-timey record player. Propped up on pillows from her reading nook. Sitting beside her intellectual soul mate, Owen Lowell-Kline. *Time* magazines dating back to 1987, everywhere. If life got any better than this, Ruthie didn't want to know about it. She might explode.

On Monday, just one week after he applied, Owen had been welcomed into the Talented and Gifted program at Poplar Middle School, and much to Ruthie's delight, he was thriving.

To help the class get to know him better, Rhea, their

TAG teacher, asked Owen to create an Inside My Brain board so she and the Titans could understand what makes him "tick." All he had to do was draw an outline of his head and fill it with pictures of what he likes to think about. But it wasn't that simple. His mother only read romance novels, and his father ran a paper-free household, so the Goldmans' tower of *Time* magazines saved him.

"Looks good," Ruthie said as she took in his collage. It included, but was not limited to, photos of Girl Scout Cookies, Audrey Hepburn, Brooks Brothers suits, French landmarks, Franklin Delano Roosevelt, a trumpet, Earth, and Wonder Woman.

Owen held the board in front of his face and proudly examined his work. "I might be the most interesting guy in the class."

"TAG brag!" Ruthie said, punching his arm. It was a term she used every time someone in the program flexed their fabulousness.

Owen bowed, pretending to be humble. "Busted." Then he folded his arms across his chest, thumbs in his armpits, and cocked his head. It was his thinking stance.

"Hey, what do you call a wizened old woman who has been in TAG for, like, two hundred years?"

The corners of Ruthie's mouth began to twitch, anticipating a smile. "I don't know. What?"

"A TAG hag!"

Ruthie laughed, but not for long. She had to one-up him or admit defeat. "When someone in TAG goes to Europe and can't sleep because of the time difference, it's called—"

"TAG lag!" Owen shot back. "When Rhea reminds you to do your homework, she's a—"

"TAG nag!" Ruthie shouted. Then, "What do you call a flexible container that—"

"A TAG bag!"

Dang, he was good.

Ruthie lifted a scrap of white paper off her carpet and waved it in the air.

"What are you doing?"

"Waving the TAG flag. I surrender. You win," Ruthie said, even though *she* spoke the last one, which made her the victor. *Ha! How's that for strategy?*

"Good job, m'lady," Owen said, though his attention had shifted to the corkboard above Ruthie's desk. Specifically, to the picture of her with two lollipop sticks poking out of her mouth like fangs. With her spine hunched and her fingers arched, she looked like a creeping vampire.

"I had just watched *Nosferatu*," Ruthie explained, and left it at that. One of the many reasons she adored Owen was because she *could* leave it at that. He knew that *Nosferatu* was a 1922 black-and-white silent movie. He knew that it was the first vampire film of all time. He knew.

Owen approached the corkboard. "May I?"

Ruthie shrugged.

He removed the pushpin, took the picture, and returned to his scrap pile on the floor. He lifted his scissors, then his eyes. *May I?* he asked again, only silent this time, like the movie.

Ruthie nodded.

Owen popped a dried apricot in his mouth and began cutting. He angled his head when his scissors rounded a corner. His tongue poked out of his mouth when he focused. He gripped the picture so intensely, his finger-tips turned white.

Warmth radiated through Ruthie's entire body, fanning out in all directions like ripples in a pond. If the heat were a color, it would be sunshine. If it were a sound, it would be wind chimes. If it had a name, it would be called "The X-Feeling." Generic? Perhaps. But this feeling wasn't like any other Ruthie had ever known. Until she could pinpoint it, she would give it the algebra treatment; brand it with an X until the equation was solved.

When Owen was done, he glued the picture of Ruthie in the space between Martin Luther King Jr. and Taylor Swift. "Voilà!"

The X-Feeling intensified. "I made the brain board?"

Owen drew back his head. "Why wouldn't you?" Then, "Wouldn't I make yours?"

"Yes!" Ruthie exclaimed. Because absolutely he would. They did their homework together every afternoon and walked Owen's dogs, Franklin and Eleanor, every evening. And if Ruthie hadn't accidentally dropped her cell phone in the Pacific Ocean, they would be texting to fill the spaces in between. Drew and Fonda had been

Ruthie's best friends for as long as she could remember. She and Sage became fast friends after meeting at TAG. But Owen shared Ruthie's intellectual curiosity and love of the arts, which put him in a category all his own. *Ha!* Ruthie laughed to herself. *The word* own *is Owen without the* e. How on point.

"I love having a boy friend!"

Owen's cheeks flushed pink. "You do?"

Ruthie scooted closer and swatted him on the leg. "Of course. Don't you?"

Owen's pink cheeks turned red. "Uh . . ."

"Don't you love having a *girl* friend?"

Owen moved his brain board to the side and smoothed his Lego figurine side part. "I do love it."

"Good," Ruthie said. "Me too."

"Me too," Owen said again.

"Me too," Ruthie also said again.

It was Owen's turn to speak, but he grinned instead. It was a stiff grin. A stunned grin. An X-grin.

Maybe the dried fruit gave him a gas cramp. "Are you oka—"

Suddenly, Owen leaned forward, and an unexpected

force pressed against Ruthie's lips and stopped her from speaking. It was soft yet urgent and smelled like apricots. It was Owen's mouth!

Heart racing, Ruthie quickly turned her face to the side and scooted backward. "What are you doing?"

Owen stood up and splayed his hands. "I—I'm so sorry," he said, pacing. "You said I was your boyfriend. I didn't know what to do. Or what you wanted me to do. Or what I was supposed to do. So I—" He knocked himself in the forehead. "Ugh! I'm so dense. I just thought—"

"It's okay," Ruthie said, trying her best to sound calm even though her entire nervous system was short-circuiting. "It was a misunderstanding. But for the record, I meant I love having a friend that's a boy. Not a *boy*friend."

"Yeah, I get that *now*," Owen scoffed. "But, ugh! I'm so sorr—"

"It's fine." Ruthie stood and placed a friendly hand on his shoulder. "I totally get how you thought that."

He slowly lifted his gaze. "You do?"

Ruthie nodded.

Owen exhaled. "What a relief."

"A relief that I forgive you, or a relief that I don't want a boyfriend?" she asked, not quite sure what she wanted his answer to be.

Owen wiggled out from under her grip. "Both. I love having you as my girl *friend*, but the whole girlfriend thing?" He shook his head. "Yeah, no thanks."

"Yeah, super no thanks."

"Yeah, super-duper no thanks."

"Yeah," Ruthie said. "I'm glad we can be honest with each other."

"That's what boy *friends* are for." Owen beamed.

"And girl friends," Ruthie added.

"Yeah. And girl *friends*."

Ruthie and Owen exchanged an all-is-forgiven smile that erased the awkwardness and deepened their bond. They had spoken their truths and come out stronger for it. How mature was *that*?

They spent the next thirty minutes cutting and pasting pictures onto Owen's brain board in comfortable silence. Every now and then, Owen would hum along to the record, but otherwise they didn't say much. *That's* how close they were. They didn't need words.

The voices inside Ruthie's head, however, were at full volume. She could hear herself telling Fonda and Drew about this funny misunderstanding. Hear them squeal in awkward delight. Hear herself go on about how empowering it feels to say no when you're not ready. Hear Fonda's mother, Joan, applaud Ruthie for staying true to herself.

More than anything, Ruthie could hear herself telling the nesties how much she missed them lately. That she had spent too much time helping Owen catch up in TAG and that she couldn't wait to make up for lost time.

Because boy *friends* were great, but girl *friends* were better.

chapter three.

"WILL WANTS TO kiss me!" Drew Harden announced upon entering Fonda's bedroom. She may have been ten minutes late for their weekly Friday-night sleepover, but she had twenty minutes of breaking news to make up for it.

"Did he *actually* say that?" Fonda raced over to relieve Drew of her sleeping bag and backpack, as if the extra weight might delay her answer.

"Or did he just lean in and go for it?" Ruthie asked. "Because I have to tell you something about Owe—"

"Fonda, your room looks different. Did you change something?" Drew knew Fonda hadn't changed a thing. Twinkle lights still hung from the seafoam-green ceiling. Decorative pillows still brought pops of color to her all-white bedding. But Drew wanted to draw out her kissing story for as long as possible. Suck on it like a candy and savor the flavor before it dissolved.

"My room has looked the same for ten years straight. Will wanting to kiss you is the only thing that's changed, so spill, teakettle. Spill!"

Drew looked down at Ruthie and the snack bowls that surrounded her. "Fonda always has the best snacks, doesn't she?"

Ruthie grabbed Drew's wrist and yanked her toward the floor. "Spill!"

"Fine. So, today, after school, Will and I went skating around his neighborhood . . ." She popped a handful of Chex Mix into her mouth.

"We know!" Fonda said as she lowered down beside them. Her flannel pajamas carried the scent of her vanilla-and-caramel body oil. "Fast-forward."

Drew chewed her Chex Mix and contemplated her next move. Should she tell them that Will's front wheels detached from his board while they were skating down Canyon View Drive? That he landed chin-first on the asphalt? That she, a wannabe nurse who carried a first aid kit in her backpack, ran to Will's side and cleaned the wound while he rested his head in her lap? That when she was done, he sat up, brushed the hair out of her face, and said, "You're beautiful, inside and out"? That the setting sun cast an orange glow on his face as he asked Drew if she wanted to be his first kiss? That she said, "First, second, *and* third"?

No. No, she shouldn't. Mostly because none of that happened, but also because Drew was embarrassed. The nesties knew how often she imagined rescuing Will from various skate injuries and nursing him back to health. But lately, these "wounded Will" daydreams included a kiss.

Drew wanted to ask Ruthie if she thought about kissing Owen, to ask Fonda if she wanted to kiss Henry, but what if they didn't? Would they judge her?

"When we finished skating," Drew continued, "we went into Will's garage to get water. His garage is totally tricked-out, by the way. He has a couch, a TV, an Xbox—"

Ruthie yawned. "This story is bore-y. Get to the point."

"I asked if he'd ever seen *Skater Girl* on Netflix and he said no. So we sat on the couch and started watching it, and—"

"How close was he sitting?" Fonda asked.

"He was on one cushion, and I was on the other."

"So, there was a crack between you?"

"Yes," Drew said. "Full crack."

"Did he try to move closer?" Ruthie asked.

"No, but he tossed his water bottle in the trash and missed. So he got up to throw it out, and when he sat back down, he sat closer."

"Crack?"

"Yeah," Drew said. "But less than before."

"Where were his arms?" Fonda asked.

"Folded across his chest."

"Where were yours?"

"Same."

"Your arms were folded across *his* chest?" Ruthie asked, her eyes wide. Sometimes she was too smart to understand simple.

"No!" Drew laughed. "My arms, my chest. His arms,

his chest. But close. I could practically *feel* his heart thumping." Her stomach fluttered at the memory. "So we get to the part where Subodh drops Prerna off after the carnival. She gets off his bike, looks back at him, then just goes inside. And Will says, 'Aw, man, he should have kissed her. I would have. You know, if that was you.'"

Fonda squealed and bicycled her legs. "What did you say?"

"I said . . . uhhhh."

Fonda gasped. "You said *uhhhh*?"

"I couldn't help it. He was looking straight at me. With. His. *Eyes*."

"I get being shocked," Ruthie said. "Wait until I tell you what happened at Owen's today."

"So then what?" Fonda pressed.

"His younger sister, Baylie, came into the garage and sat between us for the rest of the movie. But I think something might happen soon."

Ruthie's wide blue eyes glistened with concern. "Do you *want* something to happen?"

"I think so?" Drew said, even though she knew so. Then she searched their faces for signs of disgust or judgment. Instead, she got a high five and a resounding "Yes!" from Fonda.

"Yes? As in, yes, you think Will and I should kiss?"

"Totally!" Fonda nodded. "I think Henry and I should kiss too."

Drew was overcome with relief. "You don't think it's too soon?"

"Opposite," Fonda declared. "It's not soon enough. We're way behind."

"I'm not," Ruthie said.

"Yeah, yeah, you're advanced," Fonda teased. "But I'm not talking grades, I'm talking life experience."

"You mean *lip* experience," Drew said.

"Yeah, we don't have any of that." Fonda looked up at her twinkle lights and sighed. "The Avas do. So does every single girl in my health class. *Including* Nurse Beverly. We need to catch up. Let's make a first-kiss pact."

"I'm in!" Drew said. Then, "What is it?"

"It means we promise to first-kiss our crushes on the exact same night."

A zing of excitement shot up Drew's spine. "Like, when?"

"Soon," Fonda suggested. "Really soon. But no pressure. I mean, if you're not ready . . ."

"I'm ready!" Drew blurted, then blushed. "You know, to start thinking about this kind of thing."

"We can't just *think*. We have to *do*."

"What if I already did?" Ruthie peeped. She had a slight pinched expression, as if gearing up for a confession.

"Did *what*?" Drew looked at Ruthie, surprised. "Have a first kiss?"

"N-no," Ruthie stammered. "I mean, what if I already *thought* about it."

"You've been thinking about it too?" Drew asked. "What a full-on relief! I thought I was the only one."

"We all have," Fonda said. "But thinking and doing are two different things. We need to get in the game. All of us. Together."

Ruthie stood. "What if we don't have crushes?"

"What are you talking about?" Fonda said. "Drew has Will, I have Henry, and you have Owen. You still like Owen, right?"

"Sure, I *like* him, but wait—do you officially like-like Henry?"

Fonda wiggled her eyebrows. "What's not to like-like?"

"I knew it!" Drew said.

"But we all have different schedules," Ruthie mewled. "It might be hard to coordinate. Should we keep it simple and say it can be any night this month? Like, if it's in November, it counts?"

Fonda popped open a can of sparkling lemonade. "It'd be more fun if we did it on the same night, don't you think?" She opened one for Drew, another for Ruthie, and then, "I know! We could do it next Saturday, at the boy-girl parent-free high school party! Everyone will be there."

"Perfect!" Drew said. Only one week away.

Ruthie bit her thumbnail. "Does it need to be a whole pact thing? It sounds so . . . serious."

"Good point," Drew said, trying to contain her excitement. Ruthie was obviously nervous. "What if we call it a First-Kiss Club instead?"

"We could make special bracelets!" Fonda said.

"Buy mints!" Drew added.

"Have First-Kiss Club reunions!"

"Wear those giant wax lips!"

"And those bathing caps covered in flowers!" Ruthie said.

Fonda snickered. "Bathing caps?"

"Old ladies love those. And we'll still be having these reunions when we're old ladies, so . . ." Her smile quickly faded. "But what if the kiss doesn't happen for some reason? Can that person still be in the club for trying?"

"It's *going* to happen," Fonda assured her. "We have one whole week to strategize and prepare."

"And if it doesn't?" Ruthie pressed. "Can that person still wear wax lips and flowered bathing caps? Can they still go to the reunions?"

"Why would they want to?" Drew said.

Ruthie shrugged. "To be part of it."

"That would be weird, don't you think?" Drew said.

Ruthie shrugged again.

"Don't worry, though. We're all nervous. That's why we're doing it together. Leave no nestie behind!"

Fonda raised her can of sparkling lemonade and said, "To the First-Kiss Club!"

Drew and Ruthie lifted their cans, and they all clinked to the First-Kiss Club.

"In eight more sleeps, our lives will be forever changed!" Drew announced. Then she smiled to herself. *Will be forever . . .*

Yes, Will would be forever. Thanks to this club, Drew would get to relive their first kiss for decades to come.

chapter four.

LIGHTS FANNED ACROSS Fonda's bedroom walls as cars passed on the street below, each yellow swipe bringing her closer and closer to the big day.

She had woken up before her alarm, which was unusual for a Sunday morning. But Fonda was on the verge of total transformation, so these were unusual times.

In less than one week, she would be a lifetime member of the exclusive First-Kiss Club. She'd be able to whisper-swap details with the Avas, feel more grown-up around her older sisters, and, of course, cement her relationship with Henry.

Henry.

Henry and Fonda.

Honda.

Ha! Honda. It was perfect. *They* were perfect. They both had brown hair, slender builds, and tanned without burning. Sure, Henry liked to skateboard and Fonda preferred beading. His clothes were loose and hers were form-fitting. But she was charmed by his goofy sense of humor and that he didn't take himself seriously. He had full lips, good posture, and came from a nice family. But most importantly, Fonda loved being *associated* with Henry. Loved the way everyone assumed they were a thing. Loved knowing that *they* knew she was liked, that she was good enough to be kissed.

Kissed.

Fonda didn't want Henry to think she was inexperienced. (She was.) Nor did she want him to think she was *too* experienced. (She wasn't.) She didn't want to take control of the kiss. (She didn't know how.) But she didn't want to seem passive either. (Her lips, her rules.) Oh, how she envied her future self. *That* Fonda had already kissed Henry and knew how the story ended. But not this Fonda. This Fonda was clueless about everyyyything.

She laid a warm hand on her cramping belly. Even her guts were tense.

Fonda needed guidance. But from whom? Drew was equally clueless, and Ruthie was more concerned with the club than the kiss. Nurse Beverly only answered one question per day. Winfrey and Amelia would make fun of her. And her mother? *Ew.*

A pillow was Fonda's only option. Was practicing on a pillow cliché? Yes, but for good reason. Pillows don't laugh in your face.

She moved toward it slowly, pressed her lips against the cotton, and closed her eyes. It was hard to imagine Henry, because the pillowcase smelled like her Arm Candy body oil and Henry smelled like, well, she didn't know what he smelled like, but it wasn't vanilla and caramel.

There had to be a more suitable option. After scanning her bedroom, Fonda settled on the clay figurine she made in the third grade. A sad attempt at Rocket Raccoon from *Guardians of the Galaxy*. It was cracked and dusty. Probably bored from years of standing beside the dictionary Aunt Karen gave her for fifth-grade graduation. Who could blame it?

Once back in bed, Fonda gazed into Rocket's beady eyes and tried to imagine Henry. Even her cramps cringed.

"I'm so sorry," she told him. "This is weird for me too."

Then she held Rocket's pointy shoulders and drew him closer.

Closer.

Closer.

She thought about the way Henry looked at her, and only her, in the pickup parking lot after their Catalina trip. Even though her fabulous sisters were there, his brown eyes were fixed on Fonda. So what if he didn't know what the yo in fro-yo stood for? He knew how to make her feel special. What was more important than that?

Fonda pressed her lips against Rocket's cold tiny mouth. She pressed and pressed and—

Her bedroom door clicked open just as Rocket Raccoon's head fell off its shoulders and rolled onto the floor.

"What are you doing?" Winfrey screeched.

"What are *you* doing?" Fonda screeched back.

Winfrey twisted her wet hair into a topknot. "Um, I live here?" Her lips were chattering from her early-morning surf session, yet she still managed a mocking smile. "Were you just making out with Rocky Raccoon?"

"Why are you in my room?"

"You stole my robe."

"No, I didn't!"

"I did." Amelia yawned as she shuffled toward Winfrey, eyes half shut. "What's going on?"

Fonda glared at Winfrey, silently begging her not to tell Amelia what she saw. But it was too late. Winfrey closed Fonda's door, and seconds later, the sound of Amelia's witchy laughter filled the hallway.

Heart pounding, Fonda retrieved Rocket's head off the floor and tossed it into her wastebasket.

She missed and had to try again.

Maybe the trick was to start small and build up to the kiss. They could all go to Fresh & Fruity after school and maybe Fonda and Henry could break off and have some alone time. Maybe she could touch his arm or share his fro-yo. Maybe they could have the talk. If she felt more comfortable around Henry—the way Drew and Will were around each other—the kiss would come naturally; she'd know what to do.

And if not, she'd pull Rocket out of the trash, glue his head on, and beg him to take her back.

chapter five.

RUTHIE SPENT MOST of her Sunday stressing about Monday. Facing Owen after the whole boyfriend-versus-boy-*friend* mix-up was awkward enough. Now she had to find a way to un-first-kiss him so she could re-first-kiss him at Fonda's party. All while justifying her sudden change of heart.

She could feel the mounting weight of this conundrum inside her body. It was as if little magnetic lies were coasting through her bloodstream. As the magnet from one attached to the magnet of another, the lies grew bigger. The only way Ruthie could stop them was to admit that she already first-kissed Owen on Friday. But that would disqualify her from the club and all the memories, reunions, bracelets, wax lips, and bathing caps that came with it. Which was not an option. Her packed TAG schedule already made hanging out with the nesties hard enough. One more separation and she may as well be in another zip code. So, no. Ruthie had to stay the course.

"Fun fact about black holes," Ruthie said to Owen as they entered the TAG classroom. She was trying to keep things light. "People used to think they were just empty spaces, but it's the opposite. They're tons of matter crammed into a zero amount of space."

Owen flashed his brain board. "Same goes for my cranium. It's packed."

"Tag brag!" Ruthie said, though she didn't dare punch him. The less physical contact with Owen, the better.

"What up, dumb-dumbs?" Sage teased as she entered behind them. She was wearing a T-shirt with a tabular display of four elements—sulphur, argon, calcium, and samarium. Below the table, it read SArCaSm.

Ruthie envied her friend's carefree breeziness. *Must be nice.*

Once seated, Rhea hit the focus gong and bellowed, "Happy Monday, Titans!" Despite her high heels, she strode to her desk with the bounce of a woman in sneakers. Now that she was dating Fonda's Spanish teacher, Mr. Dias, she had a certain joie de vivre. And the best part? Their celebrity couple name would be DiasRhea, which never got old.

"Did everyone enjoy the rain last night?" she asked, beaming.

"Looks like we have plans after school," Owen whispered to Ruthie.

"Huh?"

He handed his phone to Ruthie and told her to read his text. It was from Fonda.

FONDA: Fro-yo after school. Tell R.

Ruthie didn't know what was weirder: the fact that Fonda was thinking about fro-yo at 8:35 a.m., or that Owen had responded yes without asking Ruthie first. How was she supposed to get out of it now? Not that she didn't love their after-school hangs. She did. Especially now that her packed TAG schedule had been keeping them apart. But what if Owen mentioned the kiss? What if Fonda or Drew mentioned the Club? What if Ruthie's lie magnets got so big, she got stuck to the metal yogurt dispensers? What then?

"Everyone thinks TAG stands for Talented and Gifted," Rhea began. Her wavy black bob bounced as if it too were in love. "But I know it means Titans Are—"

Glum, Ruthie wanted to say.

Nine eager hands shot up all around her. Owen's being the first.

"Yes, Owen?"

Owen raised his brain board. "Goal-oriented!"

"Good one, Owen. We are looking forward to picking your brain board later. But first, I have a big surprise."

"It's a chem test, isn't it?" Conrad asked. He pulled a tissue from the pack he kept on his desk and wiped his perpetually runny nose.

"*Solid* guess, Conrad," Rhea said. "But no. The surprise is not a chemistry test, but it does have a lot to do with chemistry." She leaned forward and winked. "The old-fashioned kind."

"Cringe," Alberta whispered.

"Our next unit is sex education!" Rhea announced as if she had a winning lotto ticket.

Sex ed? Ruthie's armpits began to sweat. What was happening to everyone?

"Congratulations, Titans! You're about to become parents!"

The students looked at one another, confused.

Tomoyo raised her hand. She wore a ring on every finger, each one containing her birthstone—a red ruby. "In Greek mythology, the Titans were children, not parents."

"Very observant, Tomoyo," Rhea said. "But if you recall, the Titans did become parents. Cronus fathered Zeus, remember?"

"Yeah, then Zeus dethroned Cronus!" Sage exclaimed, tucking her pink hair behind her ears. "And Cronus and the Titans were banished to Tartarus!"

"I can't be banished!" pleaded Everest, who was sitting to Ruthie's right. "I'm getting my braces off on Wednesday."

"There will be no banishing," Rhea insisted. "And you'll be parenting babies, not egomaniacal gods, which should help."

"Where do the babies come from?" Zandra asked, blond curls bouncing as she bobbed on her balance ball.

Sage nudged her black glasses up the bridge of her nose. "Zandra doesn't know where babies come from," she mocked with a *tsk-tsk* of her tongue.

"I asked where *these* babies come from. Not *all* babies." Zandra tsk-tsked back.

"Good question, Zandra. And, Sage: remember, the classroom is no place for sarcasm."

Zandra pointed at Sage's chest. "Tell that to her T-shirt!"

"In the past, students have used all sorts of baby substitutes for this time-honored assignment, like sacks of flour, bags of sugar, and, most famously, eggs."

"Egg babies are not all they're cracked up to be," Conrad said, blowing his nose again.

"So, what are we using?" Quinn asked in that adorably raspy voice of his.

"Thanks to the success of last year's talkathon, the Titans raised enough money to purchase mechanical babies."

The students applauded, though they weren't entirely sure what mechanical babies were.

"These infant simulators are programmed to give you a real-deal experience. For the next week, your precious little bundles will cry when they are hungry, tired, or need to be changed. You will need to keep them warm, but not too warm. Hold them, but don't smother them. And most importantly, never let them out of your sight. Just like real babies."

"Will we be graded on this?" Alberta asked.

"It's worth seventy-five percent of your health grade."

"Yes!" Alberta said, with a fist pump. Then, "Wait, how will you know how we're doing?"

"Each baby comes equipped with a computer processor that will record and log body temperature and how quickly you respond to its needs. Basically, every movement—"

"*Movement*?" Sage gasped. "Ew!"

The students exchanged horrified looks.

"Diapers will need to be changed, but there won't be anything in them, if that's what you're worried about," Rhea explained. "The goal is to teach you about responsibility, compassion, and the fragility of life. It'll be quite the Sisyphean task, but I know you can handle it."

"Wasn't Sisyphus the guy who annoyed the gods so much that they made him push a boulder up a hill for eternity?" Everest asked.

"Indeed," Rhea said. "Any ideas on how this relates to parenting?"

Ruthie raised her hand. "The boulder always rolled down when it got to the top of the hill, and Sisyphus had to go back down and roll it up again."

"And?" Rhea prompted.

"My mom said when I was little, I used to throw my Binky on the floor, and she used to pick it up and give it to me, and I would throw it back on the floor again."

"Exactly. Sisyphus was relegated to a task that was impossible to complete. In many ways, so are parents."

"My mom said when I was born, all she did was laundry and change diapers," Tomoyo said. "And sometimes she didn't have time for the laundry part."

Rhea chuckled like someone who could relate. "Parenting can be exhilarating, but it's also exhausting. I hope this teaches you how challenging it can be. And that you should wait until you're ready before starting a family."

"I've so got this," Alberta said while finger-combing her red hair. "I have a six-year-old sister and three-year-old twin brothers. My mom counts on me to keep things running smoothly. At least that's what she tells me every single day. And twice on weekends."

Owen and Ruthie mouthed, "TAG brag," and giggled.

"Alberta, you've raised an important point." Rhea got up from her chair, sat on the edge of her desk, and began rubbing the space her wedding ring used to be. "Support is crucial when it comes to parenting. You want someone to share the challenges and the joys with, someone reliable. A true partner."

Ruthie nibbled nervously on her bottom lip. Was this going where she thought it was going?

"To keep things efficient," Rhea said, reaching for her clipboard, "I paired you up based on location. The closer you live to your partner, the easier this will be.

Trust me. I know." She cleared her throat and began. "Favian and Tomoyo. Sage and Alberta. Conrad and Zandra . . ."

Ruthie closed her eyes and appealed to Tyche, the Greek goddess of chance. *Please don't pair me with Owen! Pleeeeease! We can't first-kiss and have a baby. It's too much.*

"Quinn and Everest. Ruthie and Owen . . ."

"Yes!" Owen said a little too loudly.

Everyone giggled. Everyone except Ruthie, whose heart beat like a prisoner trying to escape.

Desperate, she began searching for an excuse as to why she'd need a new partner but was distracted when Rhea stepped out of the classroom and returned with a cart full of crying mechanical babies. "Come and get 'em!"

"Can we name them?" Alberta asked as she kissed her baby girl's bald head.

"Yes! Please do!"

"What about Atom?" Owen said to Ruthie as he gently held a sleeping boy. "You know, because he's so small."

"Yeah, I get it," Ruthie said as she poked the baby's chunky leg.

Atom began to sob. Ruthie knew exactly how he felt.

"Looks like we can kiss our freedom goodbye," Owen said with an accepting smile.

Ruthie's stomach roiled. If only she could kiss first-kissing goodbye too.

chapter six.

THE SMELL OF damp metal and dairy greeted Drew when she entered Fresh & Fruity. The usual pop remixes blared from the speakers as the after-school crowd raced to save booths with backpacks. Photographs of fruit adorned the mint-green walls. Same scene, new Monday. And yet, something about the fro-yo shop felt . . . different. Or maybe it was Drew who had changed.

"Nab it!" Will said as he and Henry raced to claim the last available table. It was a round four top, and once Ruthie and Owen arrived, they'd be six. Would they be squished? Absolutely. Just like their beautiful lips were going to be when—

Fonda grabbed Drew by the wrist. "Fall back," she whispered. "I have a plan."

"Why? That table is fine."

"Not the table, the *club*."

"Oh, good," Drew said. "Because I was thinking about it today in math, and science, and language arts. How will we know if the boys are ready to you-know-what? What if I *thought* Will wanted to kiss but he doesn't?" It was all so confusing. Drew never felt this uncertain before she met Will. She didn't feel *any* way, except normal. And now? She could switch from insecurity to confidence, warm tingles to cold sweat, all in a matter of seconds. It was like being at an amusement park for emotions: one wild ride after another.

Fonda placed a reassuring hand on Drew's shoulder. "Don't worry. I invented BUTT."

"Butt?" Drew laughed.

"Yes. It stands for Bond, Uninterrupted alone time, Touch, Talk."

"I don't get it, but I like it."

Fonda rolled her eyes like she was tired of having to explain everything, even though explaining everything was one of her favorite things to do. "First we focus on bonding, then alone time, then flirty touch, and then we have 'the talk,' you know, to make our relationships official. When all four steps have been completed, assuming the talk goes well, the boys will be ready."

Even though Drew and Will had already bonded (skating), had uninterrupted alone time (skating), and touched arms (also skating), Drew was grateful for the game plan. If anything, it would help Fonda and Ruthie catch up. "I love BUTT!" Drew announced.

"'Scuse me?" Will said as he returned.

The girls started laughing.

"Nothing." Drew blushed. "Should we get in line?"

"You first," Fonda said, already working her B. "We'll go when you get back."

Will flashed a thumbs-up, and Drew giggled nervously. Knowing that she was plotting to kiss Will on Saturday made her feel giddy. Even a bit guilty. Like she was planning his surprise party and fighting the urge to tell him.

"Looks like they're out of yuzu balls," he said after they got their yogurt. She loved that he knew her toppings.

"Oh no. What about sours?" she said, searching.

"Very funny," Logan snipped from behind the register.

Drew and Will exchanged a look. "Why is that funny?"

"Didn't you hear?" Logan looked left, then right. He waved them closer. "Our supplier gave us Atomic Sours by mistake. And bruh, they came with a warning."

Will dumped a spoonful of peanuts into his bowl. "For what?"

"Next-level tart. They'll make your eyelashes curl. Two of our customers cried, dude. I'm talkin' grown men."

Drew examined the toppings bar. "Where are they?"

"Back room," Logan said. "They've been canceled."

Drew and Will exchanged another look, this one bubbling with mischief. "Can we try one?" Drew asked.

Logan folded his arms across his apron. "Will you give me a five-star review?"

They nodded.

"With a comment?"

They nodded again.

"Fine." Logan hurried for the back room and returned with a mason jar. He snapped on a pair of rubber gloves, twisted the lid, and pulled out two bloodred gummies. They were shaped like human skulls and covered in glistening crystals. He deposited one in each of their cups. "Eat it without moving your face. I dare you."

Will eyed the Atomic Sour, then Drew. "Ready?" he said. "One-two-three, go!"

Drew popped it in her mouth and—

Oh my gaahhh!

Spikes of sourness zipped past her jaws and stabbed her brain. And yet, she managed to remain perfectly still.

Will, however, was clutching the sides of his head and exhaling in short sharp bursts. Then his neck turned so red, Drew worried his shell necklace would explode.

"Impressive," Logan said to Drew.

Still panting, Will pointed at the sours and said, "How much for the whole jar?"

"Five stars and a killer review," Logan reminded them. "Oh, and this never happened."

Will tucked the jar under his shirt and said, "Drew

Harden, I'm challenging you to a rematch." Then, with a humble smile, he added, "As soon as I can feel my face."

"Challenge accepted," Drew said. Not because she wanted to beat him again. She simply loved that they shared a secret. A *bond*.

They arrived at the table to find Fonda and Henry laughing about something he'd shouted into one of her classrooms.

"But why *bra straps*?" Fonda asked, wiping tears from her eyes.

"I dunno." Henry chuckled. "There were a bunch of girls in there. I figured that's what you were talking about."

Drew sat. "Um, for your information, we don't talk about bras all day."

"What *do* girls talk about?" Will asked. *"Kissing?"*

"No!" Drew screeched. "Why would you say that?" She cut a quick look at Fonda. "Is that what boys talk about?"

Henry stood and in a low villainous voice said, "Men don't talk, we fight." He flexed his biceps. Fonda cracked up and followed him to the fro-yo dispensers.

Once alone, Will toasted Drew's bowl of yogurt and

said, "Your Atomic Sour game is strong! You didn't even flinch."

"I didn't?" Drew said, playing coy.

Will fixed his denim-blue eyes on Drew's narrow hazel ones and shook his head slowly.

"You're awesome."

Drew's insides soared. "I am?"

Will nodded, lowered his spoon into his yogurt, and stirred.

Heat whooshed through Drew's entire body. It melted her words and liquefied her bones. She wanted to lean in and kiss Will, right there in the middle of Fresh & Fruity. But the pact. The club. She had to wait. She *could* wait. And yet, waiting suddenly felt like depriving herself of a basic need.

Will peered past Drew's shoulder and narrowed his eyes "What the—"

Drew followed his gaze to find Owen holding the door open for Ruthie, who appeared to be cradling a—

"Is that a baby?" Henry asked as he and Fonda returned to the table.

Fonda and Drew exchanged a look of concern. How

did Ruthie and Owen have a baby? They hadn't even kissed.

They began weaving their way around the mess of chairs and discarded backpacks. Owen led the way like a rescue worker, clearing a path.

"What is that thing?" Henry asked.

"His *name* is Atom," Owen said.

"*Adam?*"

"It's not Ad-um," Ruthie said as she held the bundle against her chest. "It's A-tom."

"Because he's so small." Owen beamed.

"Makes sense," Fonda said. Then, "What's the deal with its . . . face?"

Drew leaned closer and gasped. She'd once heard someone say that all babies were beautiful, but that "someone" had never seen Atom. His dark eyes stared but didn't focus. His chubby cheeks collided with the sides of his nose, and he had two mounds of "skin" for eyebrows. He didn't look happy about it either; the corners of his mouth hung with chronic dissatisfaction.

"Atom is our sex-ed project for the week," Ruthie explained. "It's a TAG thing."

Fonda gave her a thumbs-up. "Good bonding," she mouthed.

Ruthie offered a pained smile. Atom began to cry.

"He's fine," Owen announced to the gawking strangers. "Just a little hungry."

"And ugly!" someone shouted.

Ruthie swiftly jammed a bottle between Atom's plastic lips, and the crying stopped.

"He's so . . . *cute*?" Will said, trying to be supportive.

Henry laughed. "Cute? If I ever make a horror movie, this little freak is my monster."

"Take that back," Fonda said, like a protective aunt.

"What? It's not like he can hear me."

Just then, Atom's legs started bicycling so hard they knocked Will's spoon straight out of his hand and onto the dirty floor.

"See! He's possessed!"

"Sorry!" Ruthie told Will. "I'll get you a new one."

"That's okay," Drew said as she offered her spoon to Will. "He can use mine." Then she cut a quick look to Fonda. *How's that for bonding?*

Will stood. "That's okay. I'll get a fresh one."

Drew's stomach dipped. If he was grossed out by her germs, how were they going to kiss?

Just then, a couple at the next table, both wearing pineapple-print bucket hats, began making out. Granted, they were in high school, but still . . . it was full-on and impossible to ignore.

Owen gently slid Atom from Ruthie's arms and muttered, "Tacky." Fonda watched them as if taking notes. Ruthie started tying her shoelaces. Henry tossed balled-up pieces of napkin at their heads. And Drew grew heavy with envy.

It wasn't fair. That girl wasn't a nurse, and the boy wasn't injured. They didn't need an excuse to get close, and he didn't love her because she saved him. They just kissed because they wanted to. They kissed because they could.

"Ew," Fonda muttered. "Don't worry. We don't have to do *that*."

Drew grinned as if relieved. But what if she wanted to do *that*? Would Fonda think she was *ew* too? Not that it mattered. Will was *ew* about Drew's spoon. Would he be *ew* about her lips as well?

"Dude!" Fonda gasped when one of Henry's napkin balls whacked the high school boy in the ear. He detached from his girlfriend and looked around the shop, dazed.

Everyone quickly turned away, except Henry.

"Bruh." The boy ran a hand through his beach-fried hair. "Was that you?"

"Yeah, bruh," Henry said. "Sorry to, uh, interrupt. I was just wondering about your hat."

Drew looked at him sideways. Was he *trying* to get his butt kicked?

The guy pushed back his chair. "What about my hat?"

"Is it a Lid?" Henry asked with total sincerity.

The guy nodded slowly. "Why?"

"I've been wanting one for weeks. They're super hard to find."

"They just got some at the surf shop," the girlfriend said. "We nabbed the last two pineapples, didn't we, booboo?"

Booboo looked at her and nodded. They started kissing again.

Henry stood. "I'm outta here!" He hooked his backpack over his shoulder and waved goodbye.

"Wait, where are you going?" Fonda asked, sounding slightly panicked.

"Surf shop before they sell out."

Fonda looked to Drew and Ruthie, brown eyes wide and pleading. *Now what?*

Drew flicked her chin at Henry. *Go!*

Ruthie nodded. *Now!*

"I love Lids," Fonda said. "I'm in." She grabbed her bag, looked at the girls for one last hit of encouragement, and then left in pursuit of some *uninterrupted alone time*.

"BlueRas?" Will said when he returned, not bothering to ask about Henry and Fonda's sudden departure. He only had eyes for Drew.

"Huh?"

He handed her a spoonful of purple yogurt. "Try it."

Drew took a teeny taste, then handed it back. Without hesitating, Will devoured the rest—lip germs and all!

"Any excuse to get a free sample," he said.

"Is that why you didn't share my spoon?"

Will nodded, lifted a finger to his lips, and said, "Don't tell Logan."

Drew locked her mouth and stuffed the invisible key in her pocket. She would have tossed it across the room just to prove that Will's secret was safe, but she needed that key close by. Their first kiss was less than a week away. Her lips couldn't stay locked forever.

chapter seven.

HENRY WAS A head taller than Fonda, but in that moment, she felt enormous. Not in a bloated way, though she'd just put back a sizable French vanilla with Heath Bar bits and Reese's Pieces. And certainly not in a secure way. In a, well, Fonda didn't know what it was, exactly. But it had something to do with the fact that she and Henry were walking down Bay Street together. Together but alone. As in no friends, no distractions, no buffers. Just Fonda and Henry. Henry and Fonda.

S

O

L

O.

A nestie-free trip to the surf shop had seemed like a good idea ten minutes earlier. Bonding? Check. Uninterrupted alone time? Check. But now? It felt more *heck* than *check*.

"Will and Drew seem really into each other," Fonda said as they turned onto Shoreline Avenue.

"Yeah, well, they both skate, so . . ."

"True."

Nine seconds of silence followed, which was odd. Henry was usually so chatty when his friends were around.

"I can't believe Ruthie and Owen have to deal with that baby," Fonda tried.

"I know, right?"

"If I have a girl, I'm going to name her Orange."

Henry didn't say anything.

"You know why?"

"No."

"Because nothing rhymes with Orange, so no one will give her a nickname and make fun of her."

"They'll probably make fun of her because she's named Orange."

"True." Fonda snickered. "I didn't think of that." Her voice sounded hollow inside her head. Hollow and loud. Like she was screaming inside an astronaut's helmet. Her arms swung with a wrecking ball's force. Her torso felt parade-float huge. And each time she tried to engage Henry in conversation, her bigness got even bigger. Still, she kept trying.

"Dragons must think it's awesome that we make water with our mouths," she blurted.

Henry laughed a little. "You're weird."

And you're kinda boring without your friends! Fonda wanted to say. But she didn't dare. Because what if Henry wasn't boring? What if he was just *bored*? Bored with Fonda's "weird" thoughts? What if he wished she was a different girl? A girl with normal thoughts and conversation topics. A girl who didn't feel like her body was expanding every time she spoke. A girl who knew what to say when she was alone with a boy. A girl like Drew or Ruthie or—

"Yesss!" Henry said as they approached Poplar Surf and Sport. He was pointing at the mannequin in the window dressed in jellyfish-spotted board shorts, a striped T-shirt, and an orange Lid.

"Orange," he said. "Just like your baby girl."

Fonda felt a slight sting of rejection because Henry didn't say "our baby girl." But so what? At least they were connecting.

Henry yanked open the door and slipped inside. It closed before Fonda could make it through, leaving her alone on the sidewalk to wonder if he was rude or a feminist.

According to Fonda's mother, when a man opens a door for a woman, he's saying, "You're too weak to do it yourself." Maybe Henry knew that. Maybe he was letting Fonda know he respected her and believed her upper body strength was solid.

Or maybe he was inconsiderate.

Seconds later, Drew's older brother, Doug, was in the window pulling the hat off the mannequin for Henry. When he saw Fonda, he waved her in.

"Can't," she mouthed. Then she jiggled her phone and, with an eye roll, added, "Talking to Winfrey."

Had her sister really called? No. But Fonda wished she had. She also wished she could ask Winfrey how to bond with boys, how to know if a boy likes you, how to tell whether a boy is rude or a feminist, and how to stop feeling like a parade float. But Winfrey would have made fun of Fonda for being so clueless, and Fonda would feel even bigger than she already did.

Wait! That was it! She could search up *Dear Win!*, Winfrey's eighth-grade advice blog, where she offered tips on dating and boys. According to Winfrey, it had saved more couples than Noah's ark.

She settled on a post from last February called "The ABCs of Winning Over Your Crush."

1. Always Be Careless: I'm not talking about knocking things over and being forgetful. I'm saying: pretend you couldn't *care less*. Act like your crush doesn't mean anything to you. Make them wonder why they aren't good enough, so they feel insecure and try harder.

2. Always Be Cool: Hide your true feelings and never get emotional. Act happy all the

time but not *too* happy, or they'll think you're unhinged.

3. Always Be Confident: If you don't think you're rad, no one else will.

Fonda stopped reading. No wonder Joan took Winfrey to a self-worth workshop and insisted she stop posting. But then again . . . what if Winfrey was right?

The shop door flew open, and Henry jumped onto the sidewalk wearing a bright orange bucket hat and an even brighter smile. "Scored!"

Fonda glanced up from her phone, unimpressed. *I don't care.*

"There's one left in red if you want it," he told her.

"Nah. Not feeling it."

"Really?"

Suddenly, the smell of fruity hair products filled the space between them. Fonda glanced up again, this time to find a long-legged girl in short shorts with a reflective brown lob and a glossy grin. Ava H.

"Oh my God, Henry! You got a Lid?!" she squealed. "So cute on you. So! So! So! Like, beyond!" She was not "caring less" or "acting cool," and Henry didn't seem to think she was the least bit unhinged. In fact, his bright smile seemed to brighten even more.

"My old babysitter posted a picture of her and her boyfriend wearing matching pineapple ones, so I basically ran here. Tell me they have more. I. Am. OBSESSED."

"There's one left. In red."

She trained her eyelash extensions on Fonda. "You're not getting it, are you?"

"She doesn't want it," Henry said.

Ava H. went straight to step three (touch) and whacked Henry on the arm. "Yes!"

He whacked her harder. "Right?"

Maybe he *was* a feminist.

"Don't leave," she told them. "I'll be right back."

What was it with this place and hats? Drew bought that horrible green trucker hat when she thought Will had a crush on Keelie. Keelie wore one, and Drew thought Will would like-like her if she wore one too. Fonda had told Drew her logic was warped, that girls shouldn't act all into hats to impress a guy. And yet, there she was, lingering outside Poplar Surf and Sport claiming to be a

Lid lover—a Lid lover who suddenly decided to "care less" so she could get closer to Henry before Saturday night. Meanwhile, Ava H. just swooped right in and skipped to step three like it was no big thing.

"Ava and Ava are going to die!" Ava H. said as she exited the shop, her red Lid tilted to the right, beret style. "They said I was wasting my time. That they'd be sold out. Ha! Wrong!" She gave Henry a high five. *Another touch!* "They're at Van's getting pizza. Wanna go make them jealous?"

Henry checked his reflection in the store window and shrugged. "Yeah. Why not?"

Um, hello? I'll tell you why not! Fonda wanted to shout. *I'm still here!* Why were they ignoring her? Then she remembered. Ava H. used to have a crush on Henry. Maybe she still did.

"Hey, Fonda, are you heading home?" Ava H. asked.

"Uh . . ."

Heading home would cost her serious bonding time with Henry. Or worse. What if he ended up liking Ava H. back? She was shiny, confident, and popular. Then there was Fonda, a gigantic-parade-float try-hard.

"You coming?" Henry asked in that unexpressive boy tone that was impossible to decipher. Did he want Fonda to say yes, or was he hoping she'd say no? Either way, it was all too much. Fonda needed a time-out to rethink her strategy.

"Nah, go ahead," she muttered. "I have plans."

"Okay, yeah." Henry waved. "See you tomorrow."

Fonda made a finger gun and aimed it at his Lid. "Not if I don't see you first." She quickly turned away so he wouldn't see her blush, because, come on. *Who does that?*

Certainly not Ava H. She knew how to bond with a boy, how to get alone time, how to flirt-touch, and how *not* to make cringey finger guns while talking like a cowboy. Fonda, however, needed a pillow, a clay figurine, and a club to make her first kiss happen. She needed the support of her nesties and an advice blog by her sister.

And now she might also need a new crush.

chapter eight.

GEM HOUSE WAS no White House, but Ruthie adored it nonetheless. The local bead shop was owned by a rosemary-scented hippie named Coral, who padded barefoot across the creaky floorboards—the tiny bells on her anklets providing a symphony of pings and clangs that soothed Ruthie like a lullaby. An after-school bracelet-making session was exactly what she needed.

Once the girls settled into their favorite table—a low slab of wood with macramé poufs for chairs—Ruthie set Atom down on the sheepskin area rug and exhaled. It was only Tuesday, but she was Friday-afternoon tired. Still, she took the time to organize the beads—pink in one pile, red in the other, and the letters FKC off to the side.

"What if you started calling us Honda?" Fonda said as she slid a pink bead onto her nylon thread. "Maybe that would help."

"Honda?" Ruthie asked. "What's Honda?"

Fonda looked up at her, eyebrows crinkled. "Henry and Fonda combined," she said. "I just told you that."

Ruthie shook her head. "Right, sorry." Then, "And how would that help?"

"Seriously?"

"If we start calling them Honda," Drew explained, "Henry will realize they're a couple." Then she giggled. "I know! Will and I could be Dill, and Owen and Ruthie could be . . . Owie!"

"Yes!" Fonda laughed. "Perfect! Honda, Dill, and Owie."

Or *Ruen*, Ruthie thought.

Her chest tightened at the sight of the FKC beads on her tray. They stood for First-Kiss Club and would sit in the center of their bracelets—pink to their left, red to their right. But the closer Ruthie got to placing them, the dirtier she felt. How would she look herself in the mirror, knowing she strung an *F* that didn't belong? It would be like cheating on a test and then bragging about a perfect score. The victory was dishonest and undeserved. To claim it would be criminal. To celebrate it would feel hollow.

Unless . . .

If Ruthie told the girls she forgot the *F*, her bracelet would no longer be a lie. She could wear the KC with pride. After all, she really did kiss! *Ugh*. But then she'd be lying about forgetting, so . . .

Would it be easier to tell them the truth? Sure. For now. But then what? Ruthie would be out of their club, and that would be harder.

"Is something going on with you?" Fonda asked, genuinely concerned.

"I'm tired." Ruthie glanced at her sleeping baby. *Lucky robot*. "Atom was up all night."

"I don't get it." Fonda took a sip of complimentary hot chocolate. "Why is this whole thing falling on you? Where's Owen? Why isn't he helping?" She rolled her eyes just like Joan might have. "Typical man."

"It's not his fault," Ruthie said, quick to defend him. "He offered to help, but I thought I could handle it. Also, the project is worth seventy-five percent of our grade."

Drew nodded, instantly getting it. Her friends knew Ruthie was a control freak, especially when it came to school. She wanted this done right, so she would do it herself. But that wasn't the case, not this time, anyway. Ruthie refused Owen's help because when they were together, all she thought about were his lips and her lies.

"Still," Fonda said, "Owen needs to step up." She reached for her phone and fired off a text, probably to Winfrey, who was charged with taking them home. Then she added, "And Ava H. needs to step down. I swear, if she messes this up for me . . ."

"What are you so worried about?" Ruthie asked, grateful for the change in subject.

"If Henry finds out Ava H. likes him, he'll dump me and like her instead."

"Impossible!" Ruthie said at the absurdity of it all. "Why would Henry choose a girl who wears eyelash extensions and metallic clothing over you—a feminist with DIY style and incredible snacks?"

"Men," Fonda sighed. "That's why."

"Not true," Drew said. "Remember I thought Will was going to dump me for Keelie because she liked him?"

Of course they remembered. It was only a few weeks ago.

"Well, he didn't. And you know why?"

Fonda set down her bracelet. "Why?"

"Because Will liked *me*."

Satisfied, Fonda resumed her beading.

"Speaking of, we have a skate date at four thirty," she continued, her tone confident and casual.

"Do you think you can ask him about Henry?" Fonda pressed. "You know, find out if he's said anything about Ava H."

Drew nodded. "I swear, ever since yesterday, when we shared a spoon at Fresh & Fruity, I feel like I can say anything to him."

"Impressive," Fonda said. "You've become a total BUTT master. Meanwhile, I'm, like, stuck in the crack."

"We still have four more sleeps. You'll get there," Drew said. "The Honda thing will definitely help." Then to Ruthie, "So will Owie."

"Yeah, I dunno. The baby has really put a strain on our relationship." (Aunt Gayle had spoken those exact words to Ruthie's mother after Cousin David was born.) "By the time we get him down, there's nothing left for *us*." (Those too.)

"You need to spice things up," Drew said. "My parents have date night every Wednesday. They say it keeps the romance alive." She shudders. "I know, gross, but maybe if you—"

"Hey, girl *friend*!" said a familiar male voice.

Ruthie's heart sped up. "Owen?"

"At your service, m'lady." He pulled up the pant legs on his beige Dockers and sat on a pouf. His cheeks were flushed, and his forehead glistened.

"Did you run here?"

"As fast as I could . . . from the bike stand." He chuckled. "Thank Zeus for electric steeds."

"Why?" Ruthie managed. It was all she could think to say. She longed for the days when her brain was brimming with words. Now she only had one—*tired*. Between TAG, parenting, and First-Kiss Club pressure, Ruthie was stretched thinner than a bald man's hair. And yes, she knew that analogy didn't make sense. Welcome to the point.

"Fonda texted me. She said you needed help."

"*Help?* Why would I need help?"

Atom began to cry, and Owen scooped him up.

Fonda grinned. *That's why.*

"KFC," Owen whispered as he rocked Atom back to sleep. "Kentucky Fried Chicken?"

"It's supposed to be FKC," Ruthie said. "It stands for, uh—"

The girls glared at her, a silent plea to protect their club's anonymity.

"Fonda's Kraft Club. The *K* is ironic, obviously."

"Ooooh, I love irony," Owen cooed.

"Awww, look at you two," Drew gushed. "You're such a cute couple. We should call you Owie."

"Cute *couple*?" Owen asked.

"She means a cute couple of *friends*," Ruthie blurted.

Fonda looked at her sideways. "Friends?"

"Y-yeah," Ruthie stammered. "It's an inside joke."

Owen lit up at the memory. "It was the funniest thing," he began. "Last Friday, Ruthie and I were working on my brain board, and she said—"

"NO!" Ruthie shouted as she "accidentally" knocked her tray to the floor. "Told you I'm a mess lately." She dropped to her knees and started picking beads out of the rug.

"You wouldn't be if you had some help," Fonda muttered.

"She's right," Owen said, not realizing the dig was meant for him. "Let me take Atom tonight. I insist."

"But—"

"No *buts*," he said.

"Butts," Drew peeped.

The girls busted out laughing.

"Get some sleep, Ruthie. You deserve it." With that, Owen grabbed the diaper bag and left with Atom before Ruthie could stop him. Not that she wanted to. She was grateful Owen was gone. Especially since he almost spilled her secret. But Ruthie was also a little sad. She missed her boy friend. She also missed her nesties, even though they were right beside her. Or maybe she missed how easy it had been to hang out with them before her secrets got in the way.

"What was that whole *friend* thing?" Drew asked, once Owen was gone.

Ruthie got up off the floor and set her tray back on the table. "It was just a stupid joke. You know, because we're so *not* friends. We're more."

Fonda's breath hitched. "Really? How do you know? Did you have the talk?"

"Not exactly, but it's kind of obvious. We have a baby."

"Maybe Honda should have a baby."

Ruthie laughed. "Tell me you're joking."

"Yeah, Atom is making things worse, not better," Drew said. "Which is why Owie needs a date night. I say we go to the mall, buy you a cute outfit, and—"

"Drew and I could babysit!"

Ruthie's stomach clenched. The lie magnets inside her body were getting bigger. If ever there was a time to confess the truth, it was now. Fonda and Drew would laugh at the awkwardness of it all and move on. They'd still love her. Ruthie would still be a nestie. They just wouldn't let her join the club. Wouldn't let her wear a bracelet or wax lips or a flower bathing cap. She wouldn't get to go on their reunions or load up on mints.

Unless, of course, Ruthie confessed the truth to Owen on their date and laughed at the awkwardness with *him* instead. They could refer to her dilemma as a comedy of errors and compare it to a Shakespeare play. He could give her a friendly peck on the lips Saturday night, and that would be that. Their bond would deepen. Her problem solved.

"Date night sounds perfect," Ruthie told them.

She could feel the lie magnets separating already.

chapter nine.

DREW PUT PRESSURE on the tail of her board, jumped, lifted her foot, and *bam*!

"Nice ollie!" Will said. "Not bad for a ninja warrior."

Drew shrugged, as if landing perfect ollies was a skill she had been born with, not something she and Doug had practiced for two hours last night after dinner. "But coming from a pirate, it doesn't mean much."

"How do you not see that pirates are cooler than ninjas?" Will insisted. "They don't have to shower!"

"They *do* have to shower." Drew pinched her nose. "That's the problem."

"Fair." Will flashed her a sparkly smile, kicked his

board into his hand, and hopped onto the curb. Without their friends around, Drew basked in the warmth of his undivided attention. It felt like owning the sun.

"Next, I want to work on a tail drop," she said, hoping he'd offer to help.

Her phone tinged.

"I can help if you want."

Yes!

"If you don't mind the smell of pirate pits."

Ting.

Drew ignored the needy device in her back pocket. "Okay, when?" she blurted. *Who's the needy one now?*

Ting.

"Whenever you want," Will said. Then, "I think someone's trying to get in touch with you."

Ting.

Annoyed, Drew checked her phone.

> FONDA: Don't forget.

> FONDA: Drew?

FONDA: DREW!

FONDA: Knew u'd forget.

DREW: Sorry, I was skating. #Dill.

DREW: Forget what?

FONDA: See?

DREW: See what?

FONDA: You forgot! You were going to ask W if H said anything about AH, remember?

Oops.

DREW: Srry. I'll ask right now.

FONDA: Wait!

DREW: ?

FONDA: Don't tell him I told you to ask.

Obviously! Drew thought. How could Fonda under-estimate her like that? She was clearly stressed about losing Henry to an Ava and not in her right mind.

DREW: On it! Don't worry.

FONDA: Wait a few minutes so he doesn't think we were just texting about it.

Drew texted back Great idea, even though that part was obvious too.

She slid the phone in her back pocket and—

Ting.

"Sorry," Drew said to Will as she re-retrieved her phone.

FONDA: Did you ask him yet?

DREW: You told me to wait!

FONDA: Don't wait too long. And don't forget this time.

DREW: KK.

FONDA: Don't tell him I told you.

DREW: IK.

FONDA: Make it seem like asking was ur idea.

"Is everything okay?" Will asked.

"It was my mom." Drew tightened her ponytail, as if trying to keep the truth from escaping. "Asking what I want for dinner."

"You must be starving."

"Huh?"

"You were texting for a while."

"Skating makes me hungry."

Will dropped his board and leaned the tail against the curb. "Same."

Drew felt a tingle behind her belly button. She and Will had another thing in common. *Hunger!* They were totally crushing crushes.

"Okay, so, first let's get you into position." He took Drew by the wrist and guided her toward the sidewalk.

Her tingle got tingles.

"Next, set your feet up like you're going to do an ollie." Will released her wrist but held her with his eyes. "Like this."

Drew imagined the board slipping out from under her. She'd fall back, crash into Will, and knock him to the ground.

"My head!" he'd cry.

She'd drop to her knees, examine his skull for abrasions, and then assure him that it was just a small bump.

He'd apologize for being so dramatic.

She'd smile without judgment. "It's fine. I'm a nurse. I see it all the time."

He'd sit up and hook his pinkie finger around hers. "I want to see *you* all the time."

"I want to see *you* all the time," Drew would softly say.

Then he'd caress her cheek with the back of his hand, lean forward, and—

"Dip the nose down," Will was saying. "Turn your shoulders, twist them right as you pop, and aim your foot for the landing. Ready? We'll do it together. One, two, three . . ."

Clack!

Drew landed a perfect ten. (Yes, she'd practiced tail drops too.)

"Fast learner!"

"Fast teacher!" Drew beamed.

Will stepped closer and grinned magic. The yolk-colored light of the setting sun warmed his face and brightened his blue eyes. It was all too much, and yet Drew wanted more. What was wrong with her? Did Honda and Owie feel this way too? Drew averted her gaze the way one might turn away from a blinding eclipse.

"I want to give you something," he said, stepping even closer.

Blood began pumping against Drew's ears, legs, teeth . . . Was Will going to kiss her? Her cardiovascular system seemed to think so. And if he did, would she let him? *Could* she let him? According to the FKC bracelet on her arm, that was a hard *no*.

But instead of stepping even closer, Will pulled a plastic baggie out of his pocket. It was filled with skull-shaped sours—the mere sight of which made Drew's jaw clench.

"I've been practicing," he said as he sat on his front lawn. "Ready?"

Drew lowered down beside him, not sure if she was offended or relieved that he didn't try to kiss her.

She took a sour from the bag and dropped it on her tongue. A sharp zing shot up to her brain and twisted the backs of her pupils. Her tongue burned, and saliva flooded her mouth as if trying to put out the fire. Yet she managed to remain expressionless.

"Ahhhh!" Will grabbed the sides of his head. He looked like that famous painting called *The Scream*.

All Drew had to do was take one picture of Will's contorted face to prove that ninja warriors were, indeed, cooler than pirates. She reached for her phone.

Her phone!

Fonda!

She waited for Will to catch his breath and then casually said, "Did you notice that Henry and Ava H. had matching hats today?"

"They didn't match. His was orange, and hers was red."

"I know," Drew said. "But they were both Lids."

"Oh," Will said as he fanned his face.

"Do you think they planned it?"

"Do I think they *planned* it? No, I think they both had bad hair days."

"Do you think they planned their bad hair days?" Drew pressed.

Will's face scrunched up all over again, this time because he didn't understand what she was trying to say. "What are you talking about?"

"Do you think Henry has a crush on Ava?" Drew blurted. She was a ninja who had to be home for dinner at six thirty, not a skilled interrogator with nothing but time.

Will's blond brows narrowed. "Ava R.?"

"No."

"Ava G.?"

"No."

"Ava H.?"

"Yes."

Will leaned back on his elbows. "No, I'm pretty sure Henry likes Fonda."

But do you know? Drew wanted to ask. But Will quickly added, "And I'm pretty sure I like *you*."

Drew wanted to stay with that for a minute. "I'm pretty sure I like you too," she said, wishing she could tell him about her recent nurse daydream. She also wanted to tell him that by this time next week, she wouldn't have kissing daydreams anymore. That those dreams would be real.

Instead, she sucked on that secret like a delicious candy.

"Cool," he said.

"Yeah."

They looked at each other, and looked, until Drew got a little teary. If Will assumed it was from the Atomic Sours, he'd be wrong. Her body was leaking joy.

Will looked into Drew's eyes, then down at her lips, then back at her eyes, as if reading his favorite book.

Drew pulled a handful of grass out of the ground.

Will scooted closer. "You're really good at skating."

"You too."

"I know," he teased.

She whacked him on the arm.

He didn't whack her back. Instead, he scooted even closer. So close that Drew could smell the cherry-tartness of his breath.

Too close!

Drew stood. Her FKC bracelet slid down her wrist.

"Gotta go!"

"What? Why?"

"Dinner."

Will checked his phone. "It's five sixteen."

"I told you, skating makes me hungry."

"I get it," Will said, obviously trying to be understanding. But he didn't get it. He didn't get it at all.

Drew had a pact. A bracelet. A club. How could she possibly tell the nesties she chose Will's lips over them?

She couldn't.

With that, Drew hopped on her board and headed home. Which was fine. Really. It was actually better. This way, she could have the nesties and Will, the club and her kiss. All she had to do was wait four more sleeps.

How hard could that be?

chapter ten.

FONDA CONCLUDED HER report on the California Gold Rush and checked her phone again. It was 6:07 p.m. and still no text from Drew. If only she could accept reality and move on. But much like the prospectors who arrived in the Sacramento Valley after 1850, Fonda continued to dig. Afraid that if she stopped, she'd miss the gold. So she checked one more time (nothing) and one more time after that (nothing). Then she went downstairs for dinner.

"What is all this?" Fonda asked as she entered the kitchen and what might have been another dimension.

Instead of the usual mealtime chaos, Amelia was seated at a beautifully set table, with a cloth napkin spread across her lap. The lights had been dimmed, candle flames flickered, and classical music pirouetted from the portable speaker.

"What does it look like?" Winfrey removed a dish of shriveled green beans from the oven. "Wash your hands and join us."

"Where's Mom?"

"Working on her conference speech. She asked me to take care of dinner. Probably because I'm going to be in charge this weekend."

Fonda sat. "Didn't she say we were all in charge of ourselves?"

"For small things, you know, like making beds and brushing your teeth . . ." Winfrey spooned some gnocchi onto Fonda's plate. It landed in *tinks*, like pebbles, not pasta. "But I'm in charge of big things like curfews, rules, and chores."

"Mom actually said that?" Fonda stabbed a piece of gnocchi. It was frozen in the middle and shot off her plate.

"She will when she sees this dinner." Winfrey released a mudslide of wrinkly greens onto their plates.

Fonda looked to Amelia, hoping for some pushback

on the food, Winfrey's power trip, or both. But she was focused on her phone and didn't seem to notice any of it.

Phone.

Fonda checked her texts. Still nothing.

"Let's go!" Amelia said with a fist pump. "Maddox is in!"

"No phones at the table," Winfrey said. Then, "Ha! Imagine if I was really like that?" She poured herself a glass of lemon water and passed the pitcher to Fonda. "Don't worry, girls. I run a tight ship, but not that tight." She rested her chin on folded hands, prying-mom style, and said, "So, who's Maddox?"

"He's a *sophomore*." Amelia beamed.

"At Poplar High?"

Amelia nodded.

"Cute?"

"Next level."

"Hmmm." Winfrey cocked her head. "Then why don't I know him?"

"He just moved here from Washington."

"DC or State?" Fonda asked.

"Yes."

Winfrey tried to fork a piece of gnocchi, gave up, and stabbed a bean instead. "Does he surf?"

"The internet, mostly. The guy is a *god*."

"Guys are not gods," Joan said as she blew into the kitchen, laptop in hand. "Hold on to your power, Meelie."

"Great point, Joan," Winfrey said. "Care to join us? I set a place for you, just in case."

"I wish I could." She grabbed a banana from the hanging fruit basket and hurried for the door. "I left some conference notes in my office. I won't be long."

"It's only Tuesday," Fonda tried. "And your presentation isn't until Saturday. Can't you get them tomorrow?" The less alone time Fonda had with Winfrey, the better. Her kindness act was unnerving.

Joan kissed Fonda on the forehead. "I'll be quick!"

"Take your time, Joan," Winfrey called. "I've got this."

When the front door closed, Winfrey jumped up from the table, grabbed a box of mac 'n' cheese from the freezer, and popped it in the microwave. She replaced the classical music with her Hot Girls Who Shred playlist, then returned with an energy drink and her iPad. "What's Maddox's last name?" she asked while tapping her screen to life.

"No clue."

"Spell that?"

Amelia laughed. "I meant, I have *no clue*. Just put Maddox."

"Done." Winfrey began typing. "He's on the list!"

"How many do we have so far?"

"Thirty-one. Thirty-seven if you count Jaxson Redmond's six-pack."

Fonda got up to clear her plate. "Do you want *my* guest list?"

"I already added Drew and Ruthie," Winfrey said. "You're good."

"What about the other people?"

Amelia cocked her head. "You have *other* people?"

"Yes," Fonda said, suddenly questioning herself. It didn't matter that everyone she text-invited said yes, her sisters' doubt was contagious.

"Forward it," Winfrey said.

Fonda narrowed her eyes, certain that this was a trap. "Really?"

"Guess who got DJ Ripz to make us a playlist?" Amelia interrupted.

"Let's go!" Winfrey leaned forward and high-fived her sister as the microwave beeped. Amelia jumped up from the table and beat Fonda to the last box of mac 'n' cheese in the freezer.

"I have an idea!" Fonda said like someone who hadn't been researching "cool party snacks" on Pinterest for days. "Instead of pizza, let's get a candy bar."

Her sisters exchanged one of their looks.

"There's going to be, like, fifty people here," Amelia snipped. "I don't think *one* candy bar is going to cut it."

"And who said anything about pizza? We're getting a taco truck."

"We are?" Fonda said, hating herself for sounding offended. But come on, they could have included her in that decision. "What about a photo booth? You know, the kind with the costumes and backgrounds? This guy in my social studies class has an uncle who—"

"Does it come with a time machine?" Amelia asked

as she set the microwave. "So we can go back to the year when photo booths were cool?"

Winfrey laughed. "What year was that?"

"Exactly."

The parade-float bigness Fonda had felt with Henry was being replaced by the opposite sensation—one that had her shrinking into a teeny-tiny Polly Pocket-sized version of herself. Her ideas were not needed; *she* was not needed. Fonda was so insignificant, she was starting to vanish. She turned to her phone so Winfrey and Amelia wouldn't notice the rush of tears and then . . . *Ping.*

Fonda's heart began to speed. Through the blur of tears, she checked her texts.

Drew!

Finger hovering over the screen, she paused. One tap. That's it. One tap and she'd know if Henry liked her or Ava H. One tap and she might feel joy. One tap and she might feel pain.

Fonda closed her eyes and began muttering, "Please let this be good, please let this be good, please let this be—"

"Are you having a neurological attack?" Winfrey asked.

Fonda ignored her and kept muttering. She was teetering on the edge of a defining moment. One that would determine whether her future would blossom with vibrant springtime colors or snap like the leafless branches on a barren tree.

Please choose me, Henry. Please choose me . . .

Fonda loved being associated with such a fun-loving boy. Loved his easygoing attitude and confident mess of brown hair. Loved that her classmates turned to her when Henry shouted in the halls and couldn't stomach them turning to Ava H. instead. Because then what?

Fonda would start tagging along with Dill and Owie? She'd go from "member of a fun boy-girl friend group" back into a late-blooming Ava envier, who started a kiss club she was too inexperienced to join? No. It was all too nauseating to accept. The only thing worse than wanting to matter was trying to matter and failing. And losing Henry to Ava H. would be an epic fail.

Still, Fonda had to know. She *needed* to know.

Squinting through her tears, she allowed Drew's words to come into focus.

She read them.

Then she read them again.

And again.

And again.

And again, and again, and again. Each time, her insides warmed a little more and the springtime birds chirped a little louder.

> DREW: W said H likes u!!!
> #FKC 👢👢👢

"He likes me!" Fonda shouted with an Amelia-style fist pump. "He likes *me!*"

She waited for Winfrey to ask who *he* was, just like she had asked Amelia, but her sisters were clearing the table and whispering about who-knows-what.

Not that it mattered. Fonda didn't need their approval. She needed Henry's, and she'd gotten it. The boy she chose, chose her back!

Not that *this* was about *that*. It wasn't. Nor was it about besting an Ava or getting the kissing experience everyone assumed she already had. It wasn't about earning Winfrey's and Amelia's respect or remaining in the FKC. This was about Henry and Fonda—*Honda*.

But mostly Fonda.

(And a little bit of that other stuff.)

chapter eleven.

"LET'S MEET HERE in one hour," Ruthie's mother told Ruthie, Fonda, and Drew. Then she added, "Nordstrom's cosmetics department," as if "here" wasn't clear enough.

To Dr. Fran Goldman's credit, it was the first time Ruthie withdrew money from her savings account to go outfit shopping with the nesties. The woman had every right to be suspicious. After all, Ruthie had been perfectly happy with bright colors and optimistic prints. And now she wanted something more "sophisticated." For *what*?

"TAG," Ruthie had told her. "Rhea said we should dress for the life we want, not the life we have." Which was true, but not at all why she was about to spend her babysitting money on a new outfit. Having a date night with Owen so she could tell him her plan—to first-kiss him (again) so she could be part of the FKC—was Ruthie's actual motivation. And why not look fetching in the process? But she certainly wasn't going to tell her mother *that*.

"Take good care of my grandson!" Dr. Fran teased before they parted ways. "And remember—"

"One hour," Ruthie said. "We know."

With that, Fonda led the girls through the cosmetics section, where perfume-spritzing women polluted the air with a noxious mix of floral scents that stung the back of Ruthie's nose.

"When did scented fabric softener stop being enough?" she asked.

"Stop, drop, and roll," Drew said. "It's the only way."

"Focus," Fonda said as they stepped onto the escalator. "We don't have much time."

"It's only one outfit," Ruthie said. "How much time do we need?"

"I'm talking about the big picture. It's Wednesday. The party is Saturday."

"So?"

"So, you have three days to get out of baby mode and back into crush mode. Have you even asked Owen to hang out yet?"

"No, but he'll say yes. Trust me." Firming up plans with Owen was the least of Ruthie's concerns. When they weren't together, he was at home. Alone. "The real question is, will you guys be able to take care of Atom while we're on our date?"

Drew held out her arms. "Me first!" Her competitive edge couldn't be smoothed.

When they stepped off the escalator, Ruthie placed Atom in Drew's arms while several customers gawked in disbelief, thinking he was real.

"Take good care of my son," Ruthie said, loud enough for the gawkers to hear.

"I will," Drew said. "Don't forget, I have two of my own."

"That's nothing," Fonda added. "Try having triplets."

They strode past the onlookers, as if oblivious to their shock, shoulders trembling with suppressed laughter that they didn't release until they were behind the

sale rack in the young adults section. Then they absolutely lost it.

It was little moments like these, when the nesties
cracked up for reasons that few would find funny, that
got Ruthie into this mess in the first place. The First-Kiss
Club, with its secrets and rituals and reunions, would
inspire millions more hysterical "little moments," and
Ruthie couldn't imagine missing a single one.

Fonda began sifting through the racks. "Have you
thought about where you want to go on your date?" she
asked, keeping them on task.

"Not really," Ruthie said. She hadn't thought about
anything other than the relief she'd feel once Owen
agreed to help her out of this jam.

"My mom gets super dressed up for date night with
my dad." Drew squeezed Atom between one bent arm
and sifted with the other. "Which is kinda pointless since
she puts on sweats the minute she gets home and—"

"Drew!" Ruthie interrupted. "Atom's head is
dangling."

"Huh?"

"Support his neck!"

Drew cupped the top of his head.

"Not his scalp! His neck!"

Drew finally got it right, then whispered, "He's not real."

"Yeah, well, this is worth seventy-five percent of our health grade. Owen will be so mad if I mess this up."

"Not if he sees you in *this*." Fonda held up a pink-and-red floral-print top with ruffled sleeves and an open back. "It matches our FKC bracelets."

Drew rubbed the material between her finger and thumb and winced. "Scratchy."

"What do I wear on the bottom?" Ruthie asked.

"Legs." Fonda giggled. "It's a dress."

"Maybe for a newborn, but not me," she said. Then, "What about this?"

"*Overalls?*"

Ruthie nodded.

"Are those happy-face patches on the knees?"

Ruthie nodded again. "Too babyish?"

"No," Fonda said. "Too overall-y."

"She needs to feel comfortable . . ." Drew said. "I wear sweatpants all the time and Will doesn't care."

"But Owen is fancy, so Ruthie should be fancy too."

Ruthie imagined Owen knocking on her door, then gasping a teeny bit when she stepped outside dressed in something fancy. He wouldn't have to tell her she looked pretty; his adoring gaze would say it for him.

Her chest fluttered at the thought of being admired like that.

And not the usual swoopy flutter she got from a perfect test score or a completed puzzle. It was that sunshiny, wind-chimey X-Feeling she still didn't know how to name. Ruthie had never tried to imagine Owen thinking she was pretty. Intellectually stimulating? Sure. But never pretty. And now she couldn't stop wondering how his gaze might feel in real life.

"What about this?" Fonda asked. She was holding up a denim skirt and a baby-blue T-shirt with fancy puff sleeves. "It matches your eyes."

The outfit was a perfect combination of who Ruthie was (modest) and who she wanted to be (fancy). And at 60 percent off, it was a no-brainer. So she slapped her money on the counter, then suggested they get pretzel bites to celebrate.

Even though Thanksgiving was still a few weeks away, the mall buzzed with holiday season excitement. Twinkle lights adorned the shop windows, and seasonal music filled the corridors. And of course, no one passed the girls without looking twice at Atom, which never got old.

As they approached the pretzel kiosk, Fonda said, "That dude in the dark jeans and blazer looks like a cute version of Owen."

"What do you mean, a *cute* version?" Ruthie asked, feeling surprisingly defensive. Granted, Owen dressed like a man on a yacht and "pedaling" an electric bike was his only form of exercise, but he wasn't *un*-cute. In fact, she liked that he didn't dress like every other boy at their school, that he didn't live to surf or skate or game. If Ruthie had been attracted to Owen (which she wasn't!), his unique style would have been one of the reasons why.

"Where?" Drew asked, straining to see through the swarm of toddlers tossing pennies into the fountain and the weary moms who chased them. "I don't see him."

"Neither do I," Ruthie said. "Anyway, Owen hates malls. He thinks they're uninspired and dull." Still, she took Atom back from Drew, just in case.

"Right there!" Fonda pointed at the opposite end of the hall, where a boy with Owen's bouncy gait, slicked-down hair, and leather messenger bag was walking into the bookstore while sharing a bag of popcorn with . . . a *girl*? She had beach-blond waves, a super-short romper, and a backpack dripping in decorative keychains. So, no. It wasn't Owen, because Owen didn't hang out with predictable girls like that. And if he did, Ruthie would be the first to know.

"That's not cute Owen," Drew said.

"Agreed."

"It's regular Owen with a cute girl."

Atom started to cry.

Ruthie's ears began to ring, and her vision coned. The Nordstrom bag on her shoulder became heavy, its strings biting into her flesh. She wanted to say something, *do* something. Instead, Ruthie just stood there, stunned, feeling every emotion all at once.

"He's two-timing you!" Fonda said, nostrils flared. Her rage was real, her protective instinct profound.

But Owen wasn't two-timing Ruthie. That would be impossible, since they weren't even one-timing each other. And yet, she felt nauseated by the betrayal, betrayal she wasn't even entitled to claim. Owen didn't belong to her. He didn't owe her anything. They were friends. He could hang out with whoever he wanted. But why did he want to hang out with *that* girl? Why didn't he want to hang out with *her*?

"You *need* to confront him," Fonda said.

"No. I don't want to jump to any conclusions," Ruthie said, because what she really needed was time. Time to process this breaking news, figure out what she was feeling, and why.

"Fine," Drew said. "Then let's follow him and find out what this is all about."

They grabbed Ruthie by the wrist and pulled her toward the bookstore before she could protest.

"There they are," Fonda said as they crept between the shelves.

"Maybe it's his cousin," Ruthie tried.

"Ew," Drew said. "In the *romance* section? Buying the same book?"

"Half cousin?"

Fonda and Drew exchanged a "poor Ruthie" pout. And honestly, Ruthie pitied herself too. Not because Owen had a crush, but because he hadn't told her about it. She thought they were closer than that.

"If you don't confront him, I will," Fonda said, rolling back her sleeves.

"I can't!"

"Why?" Drew asked.

Ruthie felt a wave of dizziness. How was she supposed to answer that? It was bad enough when she couldn't keep track of her lies; now she couldn't process the truth either. "I don't want to cause a scene."

"Then I will," Fonda said.

Just then, Atom started crying and Owen turned.

"Run!" Ruthie whisper-shouted.

And they did. All the way back to Nordstrom, while the bag knocked against Ruthie's leg like a cruel reminder of how foolish she had been for thinking an outfit could make a boy adore her. A boy who was busy adoring someone else.

More than anything, those mocking knocks made Ruthie wonder if the biggest lie she told was to herself, and if maybe her feelings for Owen were way more complicated than she thought.

chapter twelve.

DREW WAS LYING on her bed, staring up at the stars she and the nesties put on her ceiling when they were eight. There was still a bit of sunlight left before it got dark, too early for them to glow. But in that moment, they seemed bright. Everything did when she was talking to Will.

"Owen?" he asked. "As in Owen Lowell-Klein?"

"That's the one," Drew said, the phone hot against her ear.

"With another *girl?*"

"Yep."

"When?"

"This afternoon."

"At the *mall*?"

"Yep."

"Wow."

"What?"

"I can't believe he'd do that to Ruthie . . ." His voice trailed off for a second. "Didn't they just have a baby?"

Drew laughed. "What do you think Ruthie should do?" she asked, mostly because she was concerned, but also because she wanted Will's perspective. Did he think Ruthie should dump Owen, or fight to save the relationship? She considered hinting at the right answer—the one that would prove Will was an in-it-for-the-long-haul kind of guy. But this was a test of Will's character; he'd have to pass on his own.

"Ruthie should talk to Owen," he finally said. "Find out what the deal is."

Drew smiled to herself. "Agreed!"

"I mean, why would Owen sneak around? They're not married or anything. If he didn't want to hang out with Ruthie, why didn't he dump her?"

Drew shot up. "So sneaking around is okay when you're married? Is that what you're saying?"

"Yeah," Will said. "If you're a total scumbag, and I don't think Owen's a scumbag. Does he dress like an accountant? Yeah. But so does my dad, and he's a solid dude."

"Your dad is an *accountant*?"

"No."

Drew laughed and thought about telling Will that she and Doug turned their broken skateboards into art, that they hung them on their bedroom walls with leather straps, that she was admiring them right now. But that had nothing to do with their conversation. It was just something she wanted him to know. Instead, she said, "Dragons must think it's awesome that we make water with our mouths," curious if Will, like Henry, thought it was a weird thing to say. If he did, Drew could tell Fonda that Henry wasn't the only guy with a limited imagination—that all guys were limited.

"Maybe they don't think it's awesome," he said.

Oh no . . .

"Maybe dragons feel bad for us."

"Bad for us? Why?"

"Because mouth-water is the reason we can't make fire."

"True!" Drew beamed. "But mouth-water is a good thing."

"Why?"

"We couldn't kiss dragons without it. Our faces would melt."

Will chuckled. "Speaking of melting faces—"

Bing-bonnng.

Drew's heart began to pound. She liked being home alone, but when an unexpected rando was ringing her doorbell, not so much.

"Someone's here," she whispered.

"Where?" Will whispered back.

"At my house."

"So? There are people at my house all the time."

"No! At the door."

"Answer it."

"I'm alone," Drew muttered. "What if it's a murderer?"

"I'll stay on the phone. If it's a murderer, scream 'Dragon!' and I'll call 9-1-1."

Drew crept down the stairs, opened the door, and gasped.

Will?

He was standing on her WELCOME mat, smiling, with his phone pressed against his ear. "Surprise."

Heat burbled beneath the surface of Drew's skin. Her cells smiled. "What are you doing here?"

They each disconnected the call at the same time.

"Speaking of melting faces," Will said, picking up where he left off. "I wanted to show you something." He set down his backpack and pulled out the mason jar of Atomic Sours. What was once full was almost empty now. "Rematch," he said. "I've been practicing. Ready? One . . . two . . . three!"

They each popped an Atomic Sour in their mouths.

Will's eyes watered, but his face was perfectly still. "No problem."

"Nice!" Drew said.

"Thanks." The corners of Will's denim-blue eyes crinkled a little.

Drew's heart crinkled back.

Then Will stepped closer.

And closer.

Until they were toe to toe.

Drew's knees felt weak. Her skin began to tingle. Her cheeks burned. Something big was happening. Something magical. But no. It couldn't. Not *now*. Big magical somethings were supposed to take place on Saturday. She had to stop it. Had to wait. And yet . . .

Drew stepped closer.

Will leaned in.

Drew leaned in.

And in and in and in until Will's eyes blurred into one giant eye that made him look like a cyclops.

Drew closed her eyes.

Will closed his eye.

Will's lips met hers.

They parted.

Drew's parted.

Will's cherry-flavored tongue poked into her mouth and—

Ew!

Drew pulled back.

"Are you okay?" Will asked.

Yeah, but you aren't! Drew wanted to say. Because, *Ugh!* Something was wrong with his tongue. Like, seriously wrong.

Were all tongues bumpy? Were they supposed to feel like they were covered in tiny rocks? Was it normal? Was Will dying? Were the bumps contagious?

"I'm good," Drew managed.

"Are you sure?"

She nodded.

Looking relieved, Will reached behind his head and unclasped his ivory shell necklace. "Here," he said, placing it in her palm.

"What's this for?"

He looked at her through wisps of blond hair. "You."

"Thanks," Drew said with a forced smile. "See you tomorrow."

She closed the door a little too quickly, then hated herself for being so rude. She should have thanked him for stopping by, asked him to put the necklace on for her, promised to call him later. But Drew was kind of mad at

Will's tongue for not being the way she imagined it. Her first kiss felt like licking a construction site, and she couldn't tell the nesties. She couldn't tell anyone. In fact, Drew would have to pretend it never happened.

And the worst part? She'd have to do it all over again in three days.

chapter thirteen.

THURSDAY WAS SOGGY Burrito Day, and Fonda was all in. She transported that glistening bundle of beans through the crowded Lunch Garden and set it down on her usual table with pride.

"I can't believe you're eating that," Drew said as she unpacked her chicken dinos.

"I have to."

"Why?"

"It helps me remember."

"Remember *what*?" Drew scoffed. "That you could die of food poisoning?"

Fonda leaned in and whispered, "No, that I used to be the soggy burrito."

"What does that even mean?"

Fonda cut a look to the basketball courts, where Will and Henry were eating cafeteria hot dogs and skateboarding their way through lunch. "Just because Henry like-likes me more than he like-likes Ava H. doesn't mean I can get cocky," she said, feeling a teeny bit cocky. "The soggy burrito reminds me where I came from, you know?"

Drew popped a dino in her mouth. "Not really. But I like it." Then, "Oh no." She turned her back to the courts and lowered her head, inviting a wall of blond hair to cover her face.

"What?"

"Will and Henry just saw us."

"So?"

"They're coming over here!"

Fonda tousled her waves. "So?"

"So, I don't feel like hanging with them right now, that's all."

"Actually?"

Drew nodded.

"Why?" Fonda asked. "He gave you jewelry! That's, like, one level above 'the talk.' You're a BUTT master!"

"Shhhh," Drew hissed. "Here they come."

Skateboards in hand, the boys shuffled toward the girls like cowboys in an old-time saloon.

"Nice necklace," Will said as he lowered himself beside Drew. Which was weird. They never sat together during lunch.

Henry didn't say anything. He just adjusted his orange Lid so it covered his eyes, making it impossible for Fonda to know if he was mad, bored, or sensitive to sunlight. Before she could investigate further, the Avas entered the Lunch Garden, hair swinging as they made their way to their usual table while everyone watched but pretended not to. Ava H.'s hair was less expressive because she was wearing her red Lid. Beret style, of course.

Fonda's stomach dipped. Was it a bad dip because Henry and Ava H. were both wearing their Lids? A good dip because Fonda knew she didn't need a Lid to be liked? (Henry *was* sitting with her. He told Will he liked *her.*) Or was it a nervous dip? Their kiss was two days away and they still hadn't had "the talk"—or any kind of talk for that matter. Henry still felt kind of like a stranger.

Stomach roiling, Fonda pushed her burrito aside.

"You eating that?" Henry asked.

"Too soggy."

"Can I have it?"

"Sure," Fonda said, filling with hope. If Henry liked the soggy burrito, and Fonda *was* the soggy burrito, then Henry really *did* like Fonda. Not that she questioned Will's word. It's just that reassurance was like a salty chip. She needed more than one to feel satisfied. And right now, Fonda was craving a Costco-sized bag of reassurance chips. And she would until Henry started showing some real interest. "Guess what?"

"What?" Will answered, even though she had meant the question for Henry.

"I'm getting a taco truck for the party."

Henry bit into the burrito. "Actually?"

"Yep," Fonda said, as if the whole thing had been her idea. "And DJ Ripz made a playlist."

"Nice!" Will high-fived her. "How did you get him to do *that*?"

Fonda shrugged like it was no big deal.

Will looked at Drew, excited. Drew looked back at

him like she was enduring a period cramp. Yeah, something was up.

"Java ex ochs?" Henry asked. At least Fonda thought it was a question. He was chewing, so it was hard to know.

"What did you say?" Fonda chirped, trying not to sound grossed-out by his table manners. Maybe the burrito was hot. Maybe he felt comfortable enough to let down his guard. Or maybe she was being nitpicky and needed to relax.

"I said . . ." Henry swallowed and tried again. "Do you have an Xbox?"

"Oh," Fonda said. "No, why?"

"*Call of Duty* challenge competition, bay-bee," he said, as if Fonda knew what that meant. "My brother is in college, but I play in his league and pretend I'm him." He chuckled. "His teammates have no clue. Anyway, there's a big game Saturday, so . . ."

"Cool," Fonda said.

But was it? She knew Henry was into the military. He always wore camouflage shorts, and he had wanted to move the Seventh-Grade Slopover to Camp Pendleton instead of Catalina Island. But was he seriously asking if he could play *Call of Duty* at her party?

"Hey," Ava H. said as she passed their table, flaunting her red Lid like an engagement ring. "I'm super stoked for Saturday. Boys are going, right?"

"I am," Will said. "Henry has plans with his girlfriend."

Ava H. bristled. "You have a girlfriend?"

Fonda's insides began to tingle. If Henry said yes, it would prove that he was proud to be associated with her. She could relax when they were together and stop wondering how he felt all the time. She could skip "the talk" and trust that he'd want to kiss her on Saturday night. But what if he said no?

"Yes, Henry has a girlfriend," Will said, speaking for him. "Her name is Xbox."

Ava H.'s expression softened. The color returned to her cheeks.

Fonda didn't know the color of her own cheeks, but if she had to guess, she'd say they were a nauseated shade of green. "The talk" was definitely back on the table.

"Wanna skate?" Will asked Drew.

"Uh . . ." Drew looked at Fonda with "save me" eyes. Fonda looked back with "what is going on with you?" eyes. Drew lowered her eyes; their silent conversation was over. Which was also nauseating. The nesties told each other everything. And when they couldn't, they read each other's minds. But Fonda couldn't seem to get an accurate read on this situation. Drew's signal was blocked.

"Come on," Will urged. "Let's skate."

"That's okay," Drew said. "I don't want to be rude. Henry's still eating."

Henry stuffed the last bit of burrito in his mouth. "Done." Then, "Will said you can do a tail drop."

"I can," Drew said.

Henry raised his eyebrows in disbelief.

Drew stood. "You don't believe me?"

"I don't."

"Watch this!" Drew grabbed Henry's board and skated off. Henry grabbed Will's board and chased after her. Then Will ran after them both.

"Can I ask you a question?" Ava H. asked Fonda once they were alone.

Fonda stood. "Sure, what's up?" Maybe she needed another period purse. Maybe she wanted to know what to wear to the party. Or maybe she and the Avas were fighting and she was looking for a new friend group. But Fonda's thumping heart seemed to be preparing her for something else.

"Are you and Henry a . . . thing?" Ava H.'s voice was small and childlike. So much so that Fonda wanted to give her a hug.

"We are," Fonda said gently. "I mean, we haven't had 'the talk' yet, but I know for a fact he likes me. Why?"

Ava H. looked down at her metallic slip-ons. "I just thought that if you didn't like him, maybe I would."

"Awww, thanks," Fonda said, not sure why she treated that declaration like a compliment. Henry wasn't some flashy accessory she owned. He was a guy. A guy she happened to like-like. And that was the confusing part. If Fonda like-liked Henry so much, why did she love-love that Ava H. liked him too?

"*Thanks?*" Ava H. said, also confused by Fonda's response.

"I meant thanks for being honest."

"Oh yeah, no problem." She gazed out at the basketball courts and sighed. "I bet you think about him all the time."

"I do," Fonda said.

But did she? She thought about what Henry thought of her. She thought about what others thought about *them*. She thought about the First-Kiss Club. Who would make the first move? If she would do it right. If he would do it right. What "doing it right" even meant. But Fonda never thought about *just* Henry.

"Well, I hope you last."

Fonda cocked her head. "Last?"

Ava H. placed a warm hand on Fonda's shoulder. "You know, *forever.*"

"Really?" Fonda asked.

"Yeah, I want him to be happy," she said. "You too."

"Wow," Fonda said. The movies had it all wrong: Popular, shiny-haired girls weren't always mean. They could be selfless and vulnerable and kind. "Thank you."

"Sure," Ava H. said. And then she walked away, leaving Fonda alone in the Lunch Garden, though she was too stunned to be self-conscious about it.

Was she more shocked by Ava's support, or the notion of "forever"? Up until that moment, "forever" wasn't even a consideration; Fonda hadn't thought beyond Saturday night. When she did, she imagined swapping stories with the nesties and, well, that was kind of it.

Which could only mean one thing—Henry probably wasn't forever, but maybe, just maybe, he was for Ava.

chapter fourteen.

"WHY ARE YOU walking so fast?" Sage asked Ruthie as they returned to class after a lunch spent sketching the Santa Ana Mountains.

"I'm not," Ruthie huffed. But she was. Atom was strapped in a Baby Bjorn, bouncing against her chest as she tried to outpace her misery. Perhaps with enough speed, these uncomfortable feelings would separate from her body like boosters on a space shuttle. Perhaps they would just fall away.

"It's because you're mad at Owen, isn't it?"

Ruthie stopped and told Sage to lower her voice. "How do—"

"Well, I'm mad at *you*." This time it was Sage who sped up.

"Me? What did I do?" Ruthie asked, scampering behind her.

"You didn't tell me about you and Owen."

"What *about* us?" Ruthie asked. Was Sage referring to their first kiss, or Ruthie's attempt to cover it up?

"One: You're a thing. Two: He was with another girl at the mall yesterday. Three: I can't believe I heard this from Ava G. and not you. *Steppy*, of all people!"

"Ava G. told you all of that?"

Sage held her phone in front of Ruthie's face, inviting her to read her stepsister's texts, sent at 11:17 a.m. that day.

STEPPY: FYI your friend with the bangs saw her boyfriend with another girl at the mall yesterday. They were kissing and sharing pretzel bites. Bangs was so mad she threw popcorn at him. Love her.

SAGE: BOYFRIEND??

STEPPY: Owen something?

SAGE: HOW DO YOU KNOW?

STEPPY: I'm in language arts with her friends.

SAGE: THEY TOLD YOU?

STEPPY: No. I read lips.

Ruthie's icy insides burned. *Owen was her boyfriend? He was kissing and sharing pretzel bites with Mall Girl? Ruthie threw popcorn at them?* These were lies! Gossip! Fake news! But the truth was worse, so she simply said, "Ava G. reads lips?"

"She has the hearing of a canine. And the breath." Sage looked up at the sky, then back at Ruthie. "I thought we were tight."

The heat inside Ruthie simmered. She knew exactly how Sage felt in that moment. It was how Ruthie felt when she saw Owen with Mall Girl. Like a fool for thinking she was important. "We *are* tight. I was going to tell you as soon as we were alone."

"That's what I thought," Sage said, with a satisfied smile. "And for the record, that philandering heartbreaker is dead to me."

Ruthie opened her mouth, intending to defend Owen's honor. He was a lot of things, but philanderer wasn't one of them. They weren't a couple, so, technically, Owen hadn't been unfaithful. Not that Ruthie said that. She didn't say anything. Regardless of their status, Owen had hurt her. Maybe she deserved it for lying, but still, she was too down to stand up.

Thankfully, the fifth-period gong rang. The conversation was over.

In class, Rhea powered down the babies and waited for everyone to take their seats.

"We have a very special guest today," she began. "Nurse Beverly has been making the rounds at Poplar Middle, teaching sex education to our lucky seventh graders. So please give her a warm TAG welcome!"

Amid the applause, Owen leaned toward Ruthie, pointed at Atom, and whispered, "It's a little late for a lecture on the birds and bees, don'tcha think?"

Ruthie shrugged.

"You know, because we already have a baby."

"Yeah, I get it."

Ruthie knew she was being mean, but she couldn't help herself. Owen was free to hang out with whoever he wanted, but she still felt betrayed. Or maybe *betrayed* was the wrong feeling. Maybe what she really felt was replaceable. What did Owen get from Mall Girl that he couldn't get from Ruthie? Was her conversation more stimulating? Had she seen upward of thirty-seven foreign films? Did she win a rice cooker for breaking an escape room record? Doubt it.

Then why?

"Is something wrong?" he asked.

"I don't know," Ruthie snipped. "Is there?"

She peered deep into his brown eyes, hoping they'd tell her everything she needed to know about his feelings for Mall Girl . . . his feelings for Ruthie . . . but they offered nothing.

"Before we get started with today's exercise," Nurse Beverly said, "please write down one question you have about adolescence, something you don't have the courage to ask out loud, and I'll answer as many as I can at the end of class." She began passing around an Asics shoebox.

Without hesitation, Ruthie wrote: *I do not have a crush on my friend. So why does it bother me that he has a crush on someone else?*

"Co-parenting is like having a lab partner," Nurse Beverly began. "In order to have a productive partnership, you must share the work, listen to each other, and want similar outcomes." She sat on the edge of Rhea's desk and leaned in as if gearing up to share something big. "But do you know what's even more productive?"

"A nanny?" Owen said.

Sage glanced at Ruthie and mouthed, "Dumb-dumb."

"It's not a nanny," Nurse Beverly said, trying to hide her amusement. "It's honest communication."

Amen to that! Ruthie thought. If she and Owen had honest communication, Ruthie could ask him about Mall

Girl, their shared bag of popcorn, the matching romance novels. Or maybe she wouldn't have to. Maybe Owen would tell her all on his own. But neither of those things happened. When it came to honest communication, they *honestly* sucked.

"Let's try it!" the nurse said, as if "productive partnership" was a new fro-yo flavor. "Get together with your co-parent and take turns doing the following . . ." She indicated the instructions on the whiteboard. "First, acknowledge that parenting is hard for both of you and then get honest about the highs and lows of your experience. When you're finished, ask your partner to do the same." She tugged her ear like a kindergarten teacher. "And *listen*."

"Mommies first," Owen said as he bounced his ball closer to Ruthie.

Ruthie exhaled sharply. "Okay, so taking care of Atom has been hard for both of us."

"Yes." Owen nodded. "But also rewarding."

"Sure," Ruthie managed. Then, "So, what did you do yesterday?"

Owen looked up at the slide. "Huh?"

"Did you go anywhere after school?"

He took in the whiteboard. "I fail to see how this is relevant."

Ruthie folded her arms across her chest and glared, imagining she was an FBI interrogator, waiting for him to break.

"Okayyy. Uh, let me see." Owen shifted on his balance ball. "I went to West Coast Mall, came home, had a poke bowl, and then watched *My Octopus Teacher.*"

Ruthie saw spots. She loved that documentary and wondered if he watched it with *her.*

"Who did you go to the mall with?"

Owen glanced at his Apple Watch. "Myself."

"Are you sure about that?" Ruthie said, cells quaking, blood boiling.

"Yeah, but what does this have to do with—"

"I can't remember the last time I was at a bookstore."

"That's because you prefer library smells."

Ruthie felt a little tingle of joy. Owen knew her so well. But tingles aside, he was a dishonest communicator. Knowing her preferences wasn't enough to make that okay.

"My turn!" he said. "I acknowledge that having a baby is hard for both of us."

Ruthie nodded.

"The highs of my experience have been working with you. And the lows are everything else. What are your highs and lows?"

"Same."

Owen cocked his head. "Are you sure everything is okay?"

Ruthie stiffened. This was her chance to be honest. She could tell Owen about the outfit she bought for their date. How she planned to fill him in on the First-Kiss Club and then ask him to first-kiss her (again) at Fonda's party. How they were supposed to laugh at the absurdity of it all, but everything changed when she saw him with Mall Girl. Instead, Ruthie said, "Everything is fine."

Was she aware that she demanded honest communication from Owen, but not herself? Yes. But a classroom was no place for an elaborate confession. At least, that's what she told herself.

Rhea rang the gong, and Nurse Beverly continued with her lesson. Not that Ruthie heard a word of it. Her emotions were too loud, the pitying looks from Sage, Alberta, Tomoyo, Conrad, Everest, and Zandra too distracting. Sage must have told them that Owen was two-timing her, which made Ruthie feel even worse. Owen deserved the cold shoulder, but his reputation did not.

"And now, your questions." Nurse Beverly pulled a piece of paper out of the shoebox and read: "'My friend's boyfriend is hanging out with another girl behind her back. She should dump him, right?'"

Owen leaned toward Ruthie and whispered, "Alberta?"

Ignoring him, Ruthie cut a look to Sage, who was innocently twirling one of her pink pigtails. "You're welcome," she mouthed.

"Great question," Nurse Beverly said. Rhea nodded in agreement. "Adolescence is a tough time to be in a relationship because you're going through so many changes. I encourage students to take things slow and really get to know each other before—"

"They know each other, and he's still cheating," Sage said, disregarding the whole anonymous thing.

Owen leaned toward Ruthie again. "Zandra?"

Ruthie shrugged.

"At your age, this probably means the boy is in over his head and wants to end things, but he doesn't know how to communicate that. Your friend might take the rejection personally. Let her know that feelings aren't facts. Just because she *feeeeels* unworthy doesn't mean she *is* unworthy."

Ruthie raised her hand. "How do you know when a feeling is a fact?"

"Ah, wonderful question," Nurse Beverly said. "And my answer is, you don't. Feelings feel real in the moment, but they are fickle and fleeting. So don't act on anything right away. Give every situation twenty-four hours and then reevaluate. Ask yourself if the thing you're worried about today will matter next week. Next month. Next year. If the answer is no, let it go."

Ruthie took a moment to consider this. If Owen was still hanging out with Mall Girl next week, would it matter?

Yes. Because that would mean seven more days of secrecy and lies.

If they were hanging out next month, would it matter?

Yes. Because Owen would have less time for Ruthie, and she would miss riding on the back of his e-bike. She would miss studying with him, watching movies with him, and being called m'lady.

If Owen and Mall Girl were still hanging out next year, would it matter?

Ruthie wasn't sure about this one. By then, she and Owen would have drifted apart. They'd be used to not hanging out. Maybe she wouldn't even miss him anymore.

Ruthie gasped. The idea of *not* missing Owen made her miss him so much, it was hard to breathe. That wasn't a feeling. It was a fact.

"Do you have any other questions on this topic?" Nurse Beverly asked.

"No," Ruthie said. But she did have an answer.

The X-Feeling was not some mysterious sensation made of sunshine and wind chimes. It was affection, attraction, infatuation. It meant that Ruthie still wanted Owen to be her boy friend.

Minus the space.

chapter fifteen.

FOR DREW, THE end of math class was usually cause for celebration. Today, it was cause for stomach acid.

Before last night's kissaster, she had always gone out of her way to see Will between classes. Now, still reeling from their pact-breaking kiss, his bumpy tongue, and their unwelcome interaction at lunch, Drew was desperate to avoid him.

There was a moment earlier that day—specifically when she and Will were laughing as they skated away from Henry—when Drew thought she could get out of her tongue funk. Then her wheels rolled over a smattering of pebbles and the bumpy ride brought her right back.

And the worst part? Drew was trying to avoid Fonda

too. During lunch, the nestie obviously sensed that Drew was hiding something. And she was right! The only thing worse than being grossed out by her crush was being grossed out by her crush and not being able to tell her best friends.

Drew counted to three and slipped into the crowded hallway, making a run for it. Head down, she weaved through the foot traffic until she felt a tug on the hood of her sweatshirt.

Her breath hitched.

"What are you *doing*?"

It was Fonda.

Drew peered down at her checkered Vans, over at the water fountain, through the bustling crowd . . . anywhere but at those all-knowing eyes.

"I'm going to social studies. Why?" she said to the floor.

"You're all zigzaggy."

"That's because I was . . . eavesdropping."

"Eavesdropping?" Fonda giggle-snorted. "Why?"

"Your party is two days away. I wanted to know if anyone was talking about it."

Drew's stomach acid churned. It was the worst explanation ever, but she was too ashamed to admit that like-like hormones got the best of her, that she couldn't wait three days to kiss Will, that she lacked self-control and had disqualified herself from their pact. Those facts were like UGG slippers—best kept inside.

"Well?" Fonda asked.

"Well, what?"

"Was anyone talking about it?"

"No, which is weird, since it's two days away. What if no one shows up? Maybe you should cancel it."

"Cancel it?" Fonda said, but not in the "are you kidding me?" sort of way Drew expected. Her tone had a contemplative quality to it, like canceling might solve a problem Drew didn't know Fonda had. "You think we should?"

"Uh . . ." Drew considered making a strong case for canceling, but Fonda had been looking forward to this party all week. Everyone had. That would be too selfish, too mean—even for a hormonal pact-breaker like her. "I think you should do it. People will show up."

"Yeah," Fonda said as she double-checked her text

invite. "Not a single thumbs-down." She held the screen in front of Drew's face. "See?" Then, with the slightest trace of disappointment, she added, "I don't think we can get out of it, even if we wanted to."

"Do you want to?" Drew dared.

"No," Fonda said, a little too quickly. "Why? Do you?"

"Nope." Drew averted her eyes and checked the hall. Still no sign of Will. But he would be there eventually. "Come on, we better get to class."

Fonda checked her phone. "We have three minutes."

"Yeah, three minutes to get a good seat."

"We've had the same seats all year." Fonda grabbed Drew by the shoulders. "Okay, that's enough. Spill it."

Drew ran her fingers along Will's shell necklace, then *ugh!* That was bumpy too! "Spill *what*?"

"You've been acting weird all day."

Drew's hands became clammy as she considered telling Fonda the truth. But what was she supposed to say? That she put Will's lips before her friendships?

Desperate to gather her thoughts, Drew considered fake fainting, when Nurse Beverly appeared from the TAG corridor, surrounded by students.

Sunglasses on and Asics shoebox pressed against her torso, she had the determined stride of a celebrity trying to make a quick exit. "Get to class, everyone! I'll be back tomorrow. We'll have plenty of time for more Awk-Talk then."

"Cringe," Fonda said.

"Yeah," Drew agreed. "The anonymous question thing is cool, but that name . . ."

When the gaggle refused to let up, Nurse Beverly slipped into the girls' bathroom. The students were about to follow her inside when the sixth-period bell rang.

"I have to pee," Drew said, hoping the nurse had come across a bumpy-tongued patient and might know what to do.

"Now?"

"The bladder wants what the bladder wants. Meet you in class."

✄

Nurse Beverly was at the mirror applying bronzer to her already-bronzed face. Without hesitation, Drew claimed the sink beside her and began washing her hands.

"I want to be a nurse when I'm older."

Nurse Beverly found Drew's reflection and grinned. "Is that so?"

"I like knowing what's happening inside our bodies, and how to fix them when they break." Drew left out the part about wanting to save cute boys and having them fall in love with her; Beverly was a nurse, not a therapist.

"Those are wonderful reasons. There's nothing more rewarding than helping hurt people feel better."

"I can imagine," Drew said, because she literally did. Several times a week. "Have you ever treated someone you like?"

Nurse Beverly's kind smile revealed a row of Tic Tac–white teeth. "I like all of my patients."

"No, I mean *like*-like." Drew blushed.

"As a matter of fact . . ." The nurse got a far-off look in her eyes. "When I was five, my best friend was a boy named Calvin." She grinned at the memory. "One day, we were playing tag on my driveway and *bam!* Calvin tripped over his shoelace and skinned his knee. Blood was dripping down his leg, he was crying, and—" She paused. "Do you want to know the bizarre part?"

Drew nodded.

"I couldn't wait to clean the wound. And that's when I knew . . ."

"That you loved Calvin?"

"No." She laughed. "It's when I knew I had the power to make people feel better. And I was going to use that power as often as I could."

"Was Calvin so grateful you helped him? Did he tell you he loved you?" Drew asked, joking but not.

Nurse Beverly snickered. "No. Calvin was so offended that I gave him a Hello Kitty Band-Aid, he ran off without so much as a thank-you." She cut a look to the sink. "You really like washing your hands, don't you?"

Drew shut off the water. "Germs," she said as if that explained it all.

"I wish more kids were like you. It would slow the spread of so many viruses."

She dropped her compact in her makeup bag and zipped it shut. "Well, it was nice talking to—"

"Have you ever had a patient with a bumpy tongue?" Drew blurted.

"A what?"

"Little bumps. On a tongue. Is it normal?"

"Normal? What's normal? Every *body* is different. Do you want me to take a look?"

"No! It's not me, it's my friend."

"He could have cold sores or a fungus or a food allergy. I recommend a visit to the dentist."

Drew bristled. "How did you know it was a *he*?"

She winked. "Nurse's intuition." She hooked her bag over her shoulder, lifted her shoebox, and grinned. "You'll have it too someday."

"I hope so," Drew said, sad to see Nurse Beverly leave. It was the first sincere interaction she'd had all day.

Drew made her way down the empty corridor, wondering how she'd succeed as a nurse when she couldn't make peace with a silly, bumpy tongue. Then again, she wouldn't be kissing her patients, would she?

Ugh.

Everything would be fine if she hadn't broken the pact and kissed Will. Now Drew was doomed to a life of shame, lies, and regret. Sure, she could try to forget about last night and kiss Will all over again on Saturday. Then she could tell the nesties about his bumps, join the FKC club, and . . .

Then what?

Tell Will she just wanted to be friends? *It's not you, it's your tongue . . .*

But Drew *liked* Will.

She liked *Dill*.

At least she had. Now the "Dill" no longer made her insides flutter. Nor did it inspire romantic daydreams. Now, when Drew thought about Dill, only one thing came to mind—without the "D" he was just plain *ill*.

chapter sixteen.

TYPICALLY, FRIDAY NIGHTS were for feasting on
sleepover staples—pineapple pizza at Drew's or takeout
from the Falafel Factory at Ruthie's. But Winfrey and Amelia were firming up the details for tomorrow's party over
dinner—a dinner that Joan was once again too busy to
prepare—and they actually invited Fonda. After a lifetime
of wanting to be included, she didn't want to miss a thing.

At the same time, Fonda kind of wanted to miss all
of it—the kiss, the party, the pressure . . .

All.

Of.

It.

Yesterday, when Drew (weirdly) suggested canceling

the party, the dark parts of Fonda's brain lit up. Up until then, she had kept those parts hidden, afraid to look, afraid she'd find an insecure girl too scared to go through with all of it. And then, *bam!* Drew switched on the light and all Fonda saw was a way out.

But she had clearly misread the situation, and now here she was. Sitting down at the table with her sisters to plan the night that would change her life forever. By the end of the weekend, Fonda would have kissed Henry. She would be part of an exclusive club with her nesties. She would be able to participate in hushed debates about mouth breathing versus nose breathing with the Avas. She would go down in seventh-grade history as the girl who had access to high school house parties, cool DJs, and taco trucks. She would be just like her sisters. So, Fonda tucked her scared self back into the dark corner of her brain and tried to focus on the positive.

"What *is* this?" she asked, eyeing the mysterious blue nuggets on her plate.

"Potatoes," Winfrey said with a flick of her butterscotch-colored highlights.

"Aren't potatoes white?"

Winfrey wiped her hands on her *Your Opinion Was Not in the Recipe* apron and sat. "I put a dash of food coloring on them. Cute, right? Dig in."

"I have a stomachache," Fonda groaned, because she really did. Despite her attempt at positivity, her lower abdomen had been knotted up ever since her chat with Ava H. in the Lunch Garden. How could it not be?

Ava H.'s glitter-framed eyes sought out Henry like a searchlight. She liked him so much, she was happy he chose Fonda, so long as he was happy. But *was* Henry happy?

He seemed to enjoy their after-school group hangs. They laughed together. He let Fonda walk with him to buy his Lids. He sat with her during lunch yesterday. But was Henry *happy*? Was Fonda?

Sure, she *liked* Henry. He was funny, easygoing, and had a face for Instagram. But she didn't like-like him. Certainly not the way Ava H. did.

Her stomach cramp intensified. Were Fonda's insides trying to show her outsides what they didn't want to see? That when she feels like a gigantic parade float around a boy, he's not the right boy? When she invites him to a party and he'd rather play *Call of Duty*, he's not the right boy? And when he goes to a pizza place with Ava H. and leaves Fonda standing on a street corner, HE'S NOT THE RIGHT BOY!

And who wants to first-kiss not-the-right-boy?

Her stomach cramped again. Another message. This one urging her to put a stop to the First-Kiss Club. But how? By telling Drew and Ruthie that she changed her mind about Henry? That she wasn't ready? That she was fine being the only girl in her grade who hasn't kissed a boy? No. She could barely admit those things to herself.

Maybe Joan would know what to do. Sure, her mother was single. But the woman must have *some* experience with boys. Like back in high school or something.

Fonda stood.

"Where are *you* going?" Amelia asked, clearly not wanting to be the only one left to eat Winfrey's food.

"I need to talk to Mom."

"Joan is rehearsing her speech and doesn't want to be disturbed," Winfrey said. "I'm in charge." She leaned back in her chair. "Is there anything *I* can help you with?"

Short of canceling the party and giving Fonda the

perfect excuse to call off this pact, the answer was no. And Winfrey would never cancel her party. But what if Fonda could make Winfrey cancel *her*?

"Yeah, there is something you can help me with." Fonda sat. "You could learn how to cook."

Winfrey gasped.

"Did you seriously just say that?" Amelia's tone was one part shock, two parts awe.

"Yeah, I said that, Amelia. Someone had to. Now, how about we toss these blue Smurf turds and get down to business, starting with that taco truck. I mean, beans at a party? The DJ won't be the only one who Ripz."

Eyebrows arched; her sisters exchanged a familiar look. It meant they were going to unleash their wrath on Fonda, and for the first time ever, she was thrilled.

"The good news is," Fonda continued, "I invited Magnificent Mitch, and he's in!"

"Who's Magnificent Mitch?"

"The best magician in Orange County, and get this, he's only thirteen!"

"Dude!" Winfrey stood and put her hands on her hips. "If you honestly think—"

"Don't worry, he's not going to charge us. I told him it was a fundraiser." Fonda got up and cleared her plate. "That reminds me. We need three pounds of romaine lettuce for his rabbits. Organic only. Can one of you pick that up in the morning?"

"Done!" Winfrey said.

"Thanks," Fonda said, ignoring her sister's flared nostrils. "Is there any dessert?"

"No, Fondle. I meant *you're* done. As in tell that baby magician that the party is canceled. And by party, I mean you, Fonda. You and your friends are off the list. You're canceled."

"Can-celed," Amelia echoed.

"*What?*" Fonda forced her mouth into a frown and let out a sad little whine. "You can't do that!"

"Too late." Amelia adjusted the red straps on her bikini top. "We already did."

"And don't even *try* telling Joan unless you want the entire universe to know you were making out with Rocket Raccoon."

"That's so uncool!" Fonda managed.

"No, *you're* uncool," Winfrey said.

"And you're *mean!*" Fonda stomped up to her bedroom and slammed her door.

Annnnd cut!

Fonda's heart may have been pounding, but her soul smiled as she collapsed onto her bed, all of her problems solved. Now she wouldn't have to pretend she wanted to kiss Henry. She wouldn't have to wonder if Henry wanted to kiss her. She wouldn't have to find a graceful way to back out of the pact. Her sisters found it for her.

Fonda quickly sent a group text to everyone on her guest list, minus Ruthie, who didn't have a phone, and broke the "bad" news.

> FONDA: PARTY IS OFF.
> So bummed. Older sisters,
> am I right? 😩

She leaned back onto her pillows with relief. It was over.

Then, *Ping!*

> DREW: WHAT HAPPENED?

FONDA: Long story.

Ping!

DREW: So . . . everything is off?

FONDA: Yep ☹ everything.

Ping!

DREW: ☹

Ping!

AVA G.: Can't you make them change their minds?

FONDA: Tried.

Ping!

KAT EVANS: Are anyone else's parents going away?

Ping!

OWEN: Mine are going out for dinner.

Ping!

TONI SORKIN: Until Sunday?

Ping!

OWEN: No. But at least three hours.

Ping!

SAGE: DUMB-DUMB.

Ping!

OWEN: HARSH.

Ping!

SAGE: You deserve it.

Ping!

OWEN: What did I do?

Ping!

SAGE: Um, I think you know.

Ping!

WILL: What about my garage?

Ping!

DREW: Too small.

Ping!

LEAH PELLEGRINO: Drew was in Will's garage?

Ping!

AVA G.: Yes, I told you that.

Ping!

DREW: How did you know?

Ping!

SAGE: She reads lips.

Ping!

AVA G.: And body language.

Ping!

TONI SORKIN: That's creepy.

Ping!

AVA R.: Party is back on!

FONDA: Huh?

Ping!

DREW: ?????

Ping!

AVA R.: I reserved a firepit at Emerald Beach. 5PM.

Ping!

OWEN: Ava is our savia!

Ping!

No! No! No!

The pinging continued, with praise for Ava R., who would now go down in PMS history for saving the party (and destroying Fonda's life).

Fonda silenced her phone and buried her head in her pillows. Now what?

Not only had she picked a fight with her sisters for no reason, but the FKC was back on. Fonda would have to kiss Henry even though he wasn't "the one." Correction, Henry *was* the one.

The *wrong* one.

chapter seventeen.

RUTHIE GAZED INTO Atom's hazel eyes as he glugged fake milk from his bottle. They were lifeless and void of, well, everything. Complicated emotions had not been built into his hard drive; feeling was not an option. Ruthie sighed. *Must be nice . . .*

After setting him down for his post-dinner nap, Ruthie flopped onto her bed and contemplated her next move. Fonda had canceled their sleepover so she could party plan with her sisters, and without that Friday-night ritual, Ruthie was lost. So when Fonda called to say the party had been moved to the beach, and that it no longer included the high schoolers, Ruthie's frown turned upside down.

"Does that mean the sleepover is back on?" she had asked.

"I dunno. I'm kinda tired," Fonda said, sounding surprisingly bummed.

Ruthie beamed. "I can keep you company. I'll be mellow."

"That's okay. I'm good. See you tomorrow."

Before Ruthie could say, *Good? Really? Because you don't sound good, you sound forlorn,* Fonda was gone. No explanation. No details. All she knew was that the First-Kiss Club was happening, and Ruthie's thoughts were tangled. If advice came in baby bottles, she'd glug ten of them. That's how thirsty she was for guidance, a good listener, a nonjudgmental confidant.

Foxy!

Ruthie reached behind her bed and latched on to the stuffed fox she'd had since second grade. She rescued Foxy from the school's lost and found, and from that moment on, it was Foxy who had done the rescuing. *Lost and friend!*

"I need help," Ruthie said as she brushed the dust off of its pointy black snout.

Foxy stared back at Ruthie, eyes hard and dead as Atom's. She had grown to expect that vacant stare from her robo-baby, but Foxy? Never.

"Is something bothering you?"

What makes you think something's bothering me? Foxy seemed to say.

"I dunno. You look distant, checked out."

Yeah, well, distant and checked out is the only way to survive around here these days. That crying machine you're in love with is a lot.

"In *love*?" Ruthie scoffed. "Ew, hardly. Atom goes back on Monday, and I can't wait." She lowered her voice. "He's a vampire that has drained all life from my soul. I'm like the walking dead, minus the walking."

Why are you whispering?

"I don't want to wake him up."

Why not?

"Because I'd rather talk to you," Ruthie said.

You would?

"One thousand percent."

I thought you took issue with that phrase because it's hyperbolic.

Ruthie smiled. The fox knew her so well. "I do take issue with it. 'One hundred percent' should be enough, because it *is* enough. It's literally everything. But that's kind of why I said it. You're everything, Foxy, and more."

The light returned to Foxy's eyes. *Tell me what's on your mind. Don't leave one thing out.*

Ruthie's chest tightened. "It's actually three things: One, how can I be in the First-Kiss Club if I've already had a first kiss; two, I realized I like Owen more than a boy *friend*, which is a problem because, three, he likes Mall Girl."

Foxy decided to tackle one problem at a time.

One: If you kiss Owen tomorrow night, it will *be your first kiss.*

"How? Why?"

Because your first first kiss was a misunderstanding, so it doesn't count.

The tightness in Ruthie's chest eased up a teensy bit. It was a solid point.

Two: Realizing you like Owen as more than a friend isn't a problem. It's a revelation! You have to know what you want in order to get it. And now you know.

"But what about—"

What about Mall Girl? Yes, that could be a problem. Foxy paused a moment. *Here's the thing . . . for the past week, I thought you were replacing me with Atom.*

"Foxy, how could you ever think—"

Let me finish. I was jealous and insecure, and if I'm being totally honest, it was hard for me to think about anything else. When I finally told you the truth, I felt better. Yes, you said what I wanted to hear, but even if you'd told me you liked Atom more than me, I would have survived. Not knowing is always harder than knowing—even when knowing hurts. Trust me.

"I do," Ruthie said. So much so that she gave Foxy a suffocating thank-you hug and ran up the block to Owen's house. *Ready or not, Truth, here I come!*

When Ruthie rang Owen's Beethoven-themed doorbell, she was out of breath. Was it from exertion, or was she having a panic attack?

"Owen, you know how semicolons bridge two

independent clauses that are closely related but not quite one?" she practiced as "Für Elise" began to play. "Well, what if we got rid of the bridge and joined together—"

The door opened.

"Ruthie?" Owen began smoothing his side part. "What are you doing here? Is everything okay? Where's Atom?"

"Sleeping. Anyway, I need to talk to you about semicolons—"

"Is that our pizza?" a girl's voice called from the kitchen.

"No," Owen called back. "It's just my neighbor."

Neighbor?

Had Owen really reduced Ruthie, his former girl *friend*, to a noun who lived down the street? The tightness in her chest tightened even more, and then much more when the girl emerged from the kitchen with two bottles of root beer and a territorial grin on her face.

She gave the root beers to Owen and extended her right hand for a shake. "Hi, I'm Mall Girl," she may as well have said. Because that's all Ruthie heard. She shook

Mall Girl's frosty hand and looked away. The less Ruthie saw of her, the easier it would be to convince herself that her long-lashed replacement looked like Shrek.

"Okay, well, nice meeting you," Ruthie said as her vision began to narrow. She turned to leave.

"Where are you going?" Owen called. "I thought you wanted to talk about semicolons."

"Semicolons are the worst!"

"That's *it*?"

She waved without looking back. "Gotta go before Atom wakes up."

Ruthie hurried to the safety of her bedroom, eager to blame Foxy for getting it all wrong. Because not knowing the truth wasn't harder than knowing; it left room for hope. Now all hope was gone, and nothing hurt more than that.

chapter eighteen.

DREW SHUT OFF the hair dryer and evaluated her beach-party outfit in the bathroom mirror. She was wearing navy drawstring pants, a white sweatshirt, and . . . who cares? Will's shell necklace was glaring at her—an evil, jagged-toothed smile that appeared to be taking pleasure in her angst. *Hey, Drew, are you ready for another bumpy kiss? Mwah-hahaha!*

What the necklace didn't realize was that Drew's pinched expression had more to do with the nesties than with Will. Yes, she was dreading their second kiss, but Drew hadn't *betrayed* Will. She had betrayed the nesties, though. *Twice.*

First, Drew broke their honesty pact by not

telling Fonda and Ruthie she kissed Will. Second, she broke their first-kiss pact by not waiting for tonight's party and, well, see above. Bottom line: Drew broke 100 percent of the nesties' pacts, and the guilt was suffocating.

"My turn!" Doug announced as he entered the bathroom with a towel wrapped around his waist and a pep in his step. Drew envied his lightheartedness—Doug moved like a guy who had never done anything wrong.

He turned on the shower, then shooed Drew away. "A little privacy, please?"

Drew's legs were too heavy to move. "Have you ever betrayed anyone?" she called over the sound of hissing water.

Doug turned off the shower. "Cheating-on-someone betrayed or tattletale betrayed?"

"Both," Drew said, because both applied. She had cheated on the nesties by pre-kissing Will, *and* she was thinking about tattling on herself and telling them the truth.

"Nope." Doug turned the shower back on. "Never. But someone betrayed me."

"Who?"

He turned off the shower. "Sara Manford."

"Your eighth-grade girlfriend?"

"Yep. She made out with Bradley Bryan during our graduation party."

"How do you know?"

"She told me two days later."

Drew imagined telling the nesties what she had done, but unlike her nurse daydreams, she couldn't picture the ending. Would they thank her for telling the truth, or judge her for losing control? Would they ask Drew for kissing advice, or ask her to remove her FKC bracelet? "It was pretty brave of Sara to tell you."

"Brave?" Doug scoffed. "No, it was selfish."

"How is honesty selfish?'

"The honesty was for Sara, not me."

Drew cocked her head.

"She told me because she felt guilty."

"So?"

"So, she felt better once she told me, and I felt awful."

"I don't get it. Do you wish Sara lied to you instead?"

"No." Doug ran a hand through his hair. "I wish she

hadn't kissed Bradley Bryan. Or I wish she'd broken up with me instead of making me look like a fool. But since she did cheat, yeah, I wish she'd kept it to herself and carried the guilt around with her like a backpack full of bricks instead of dumping it on me." Doug glanced down at Drew's necklace. "Why? Did someone cheat on you?"

"No."

"Good. Now will you *please* leave?"

Drew shuffled back to her room, burdened by the weight of her massive guilt-bricks. Carrying these lies was unbearable. According to Doug, unloading them would be selfish. So what was she supposed to do? Her friends would be at her house in fifteen minutes. Her mother would be driving them to Emerald Beach in twenty. Once there, Drew would have to act excited to kiss Will, excited to share this night of firsts with her nesties, excited to become a member of a club she didn't deserve to join. And acting around Fonda and Ruthie was akin to Drew's worn-out white tank top—they always saw through it.

Thumbs hovering over her phone's touchscreen, Drew considered texting some excuse as to why she couldn't make it. But that would be one more lie—another heavy guilt-brick to lug around. All she could do was pray.

Kneeling, she pressed her hands together and closed her eyes. "Dear Universe, please make it rain right now in Poplar Creek, California, so that Ava R. has to cancel her beach party. To be clear, this isn't *just* about helping me avoid Will and getting me out of the kiss pact. As you know, Orange County is in a drought, so technically, it's also for the plants. Thanks. Love, Drew."

Ten minutes later, Drew checked her weather app; the forecast was clear. *Ugh!* If only she could say that about her conscience or Will's tongue.

When the doorbell rang, Drew and her backpack full of guilt-bricks began making their way downstairs.

"Coming through!" Doug called as he raced by, crop-dusting the hallway with his suede-and-pepper-scented cologne. His wet hair was slicked back, and his favorite Hawaiian shirt was wrinkle-free.

"Where are you going?"

"Next door to Amelia's," he said. "Taco truck, baby!"

"That's still happening?" Drew asked, confused.

"It will be when I get there." Doug opened the front door with a magician's flourish.

"Looking good, ladies," he said as he took in Fonda and Ruthie. And they did look good. Fonda was dressed in faded Levi's, a yellow crop top, and an open flannel shirt. Ruthie had on a purple tie-dyed romper and a knit hat with pussycat ears. They were the perfect mix of beach casual and bonfire cool. And yet, something about them made Drew think of Christmas trees after New Year's—decorated but dim.

Did they know that Drew and Will already kissed?

"Night-night, ugly baby," Doug said to Atom before heading next door.

"Is your party back on?" Drew asked Fonda, though she didn't have to. She could hear the thumping music, see the high school kids on the front porch, smell the carnitas.

"Yeah. Winfrey and Amelia decided to do it after all," Fonda said, avoiding Drew's eyes. *She knew! She was mad! She was acting too!* "But, you know, since Ava R. already set up the whole beach thing, I figured we should just go there."

"Makes sense," Drew said as she peeked up at the sky. Still no sign of rain. "Wanna wait for my mom in the living room?"

The girls shrugged like shy strangers. *Yeah, something was definitely up.*

"Soooo . . ." Ruthie said as they sat on the living room couch. "Who's excited to kiss?"

"Me," Drew muttered, sounding anything but.

"Me too," Ruthie said.

"Misery," Fonda added.

"Misery?"

Fonda giggled. "I said, 'me *three*.'"

"Oh."

"Are you okay?" Ruthie asked.

"Yeah, you seem a little down," Fonda added. "If there's something you want to talk about, we'll stay home with you—"

"Totally!" Ruthie indicated Atom, who was asleep in her arms. "And this guy is a total party pooper, pun intended, so I'm fine with staying home."

Drew glanced out the living room window at the branches on the eucalyptus tree. The leaves were perfectly still. "No, I'm okay," she said, her voice an octave too high. She couldn't stand not knowing what they knew. Couldn't deal with the weight of the guilt-bricks. Wasn't sure if Doug's advice was the right advice. If she could just slip off and google *Should I admit to breaking a pact?* . . . Instead, she said, "I'm going to put on different pants."

"Why? I like your pants," Fonda said.

"No, you don't. Last time I wore them, you said they looked like pajamas."

"People can change their minds, you know," Fonda insisted, like this was about more than leisurewear.

"Yeah," Ruthie added. "It happens sometimes."

"What happens?"

"Mind changing. Like when you want to use a semi-colon but make two separate sentences instead."

Drew and Fonda looked at each other, confused.

"It's like, sometimes you don't think you like some-one, I mean, some*thing*, and then suddenly you do."

"Or maybe you *thought* you liked some*thing*, but then you realize you don't," Fonda said.

"Wait, so do you like my pants or not?"

Drew's mother appeared, car keys in hand. "Hi, girls! Are you ready to leave?"

"Hi, Mrs. Harden," Fonda and Ruthie said together.

"Aww, you girls look so bute!" she said. "Beach cute."

Fonda and Ruthie giggled politely. Drew rolled her eyes.

"Mom, why do you always do that? It's so annoying."

Her mother tightened her blond high ponytail. "Do what?"

She knew *exactly* what.

"Combine words."

"It saves me time."

Drew wanted to say, "How does it save time when it takes extra time to explain what it means?" But she didn't have the strength to push back; her guilt was getting heavier by the second. "Let's just go."

"Not until I get a pic-turrre!" her mother singsonged. That upbeat personality of hers made sense at Battleflag Family Camp. People paid her to show them a good time. But summer was over. Regular life had resumed. Couldn't she just be normal?

"It's a beach hang, Mom. Not prom."

"Present moments are future memories." She slid her phone from the side pocket of her leggings. "All right, girls. Get together."

Their friendship bracelets collided as they put their arms around one another and shimmied into position.

Within seconds, Drew was soothed by the familiar scent of Fonda's vanilla-and-caramel body oil and the curve of Ruthie's waist. They pressed their cheeks together, just like they always did when posing, and pressed, and pressed. Soon, the gaps between them disappeared. Drew was close to Fonda and Ruthie again. Bonded. Connected. The way the FKC was supposed to make her feel but didn't.

"Say nesties!"

"Nesties!"

"Perfect!" her mother clicked, then lowered her phone. "*Now* we can go."

Drew didn't move. None of the girls did. They simply stood there, clinging to familiarity. Aware that they were about to break off and head into the unknown.

chapter nineteen.

THE SUN, LIKE a coin in the slot of a gumball machine, slipped below the horizon and darkened the beach. Suddenly, Ava R.'s party seemed to be populated by a mass of faceless figures and mingling shadows, making this already-stressful night even more impossible to navigate.

"How are we supposed to find them?" Fonda asked Drew and Ruthie as the last winks of orange light faded from the sky. She hoped one of them would declare the party too chaotic for kissing and call the whole thing off.

Instead, Ruthie pointed at the shoreline and said, "I think I see Henry."

"Where?"

"The orange Lid."

"No sign of Will, though," Drew said, as if that were good news.

Ruthie stuck a bottle in Atom's mouth, even though he was asleep. "Yeah, no Owen either."

"If you guys want me to wait, I will," Fonda said, hoping her offer sounded more like a kind gesture than a cry for help.

"Yeah, maybe we should reschedule," Drew said. "I mean, if they're not here . . ."

"If Henry is here, Will is here," Ruthie said. "Anyway, don't worry about it. I'm sure he'll be here soon." She held out her arm and indicated their bracelet. "The FKC club awaits."

Drew sighed. "Okay, if you insist." She extended her arm.

Fonda did the same.

Once all three of their bracelets touched, the tension inside Fonda's belly relaxed to a tingle. So what if Henry wasn't "the one"? Their kiss would only last a few seconds, but the First-Kiss Club would span a lifetime. So why not go for it? Get it over with. Her lips, his lips, press, and done. That was it. Then everything would be better.

Fonda would have experience. A secret club with her nesties. *Swagger.*

"Okay, let's do this!" Fonda extracted a jar of strawberry-flavored lip balm from her cross-body bag and opened the top. *Ew.* It was caked in sand. So much for that. "Good luck, everyone."

"Wait!" Drew said. "We forgot the mints. Does that mean we have to wait?"

Ruthie pulled a piece of cinnamon gum from her pocket. "We can split this. But I won't eat my third unless I know Owen's here, in case you guys want it. And if he's not here, maybe I can still be in the club because it's not my fault he didn't show up."

"I don't know about cinnamon," Drew said. "It's strong, but is it *too* strong?"

"There's no such thing as *too* strong," Fonda said. "Strong sends a message."

"What kind of message? That we have bad breath?"

Fonda laughed. "That we're powerful. We're the kind of girls who speak our minds. And when we do, it smells like cinnamon."

Inspiring as it was, Fonda's spicy little pep talk made

her insides churn. If she was "the kind of girl who spoke her mind," she'd be saying, "I don't want to kiss Henry! I'm not ready. I want to wait for 'the one'!" And it wouldn't smell like cinnamon. It would smell crisp and clean, like cold mountain springwater. Like truth instead of hypocrisy. But in the moment, Fonda wasn't that kind of girl . . .

"Gum, please," she said to Ruthie. "I'm going in."

With a pounding heart and a mouth flavored with cinnamon, Fonda took to the beach without looking back, a hypocritical girl on a mission.

Thanks to the band of silver moonlight, she found Henry by the shoreline, his forehead slick with sweat.

"Hey," she said as she approached, suddenly aware that she didn't have a plan. "What are you doing?"

He ran a hand through his sweaty dark hair. "Tackle Frisbee Football." His gaze wandered toward the shoreline, where a girl wearing a red Lid was saving a glow-in-the-dark Frisbee from being washed out to sea.

Ava H. was into Tackle Frisbee Football?

"Play with us," Henry said.

It was nice of him to offer, and yet, something about

the invitation made Fonda feel lonely. Because if Henry knew her, like, really knew her, he would have known that beading was her one and only sport. But faster than Fonda could say, "How about a walk instead?" the glowing green disk sliced through the darkness, and Henry took off. Once again, he left Fonda alone, just like he had outside the surf shop, just like he had in the Lunch Garden.

But what did she expect? Henry was in the middle of a game. He had no idea she wanted to kiss him. And he wouldn't unless Fonda acted like a powerful cinnamon breather and spoke her mind.

Moments later, when the Frisbee landed back in the water, Fonda moved in.

"So, I can't play because I'm already playing another game," she told him.

"Volleyball?" Henry asked, looking past Fonda, eager for that Frisbee.

"No."

"Paddleball?"

"No."

"Boggle?"

"No." Fonda giggled. "Truth or Dare." Forget romance—the sooner she got this over with, the better. "And someone dared me to kiss you."

Henry finally looked at her. "Now?"

Fonda nodded. "It can be fast."

"Um, okay." Henry stepped toward her, leaned closer, and *thwack*. He caught the Frisbee between his palms and ran.

He didn't get far before a charge of kids, led by Ava H., pounced. Within seconds he was buried under a hill of laughing, panting seventh graders.

While Henry struggled to break free, Fonda wondered if Drew and Ruthie were making any progress. And if so, what they would say if they saw her standing there alone. Would they tell her to try harder or to walk away?

Suddenly, a familiar voice appeared in her head. It said, *When given the choice between Fonda and a Frisbee, Henry chose the Frisbee. Don't make the same mistake. Choose Fonda.*

The voice didn't belong to the nesties. It belonged to her mother. And she was right.

As everyone in the heap began to untangle, Fonda

called a quick time-out and ran over to Ava H. "Can I talk to you for a minute?"

"I'm not flirting with him," she said as they stepped away from the group. Her lashes were coated with sand instead of mascara. Her cheeks were pink from exercise, not blush. Her hair was mussed and wild. And yet, in that moment, Ava H. was more beautiful than ever—a seventh-grade girl not trying to be anyone but herself. "My goal is to steal the Frisbee, not *Henry*. Just so you know."

"I know. Don't worry, I'm not mad."

"You're not?"

"Opposite."

Ava H. knit her eyebrows. "So you're . . . glad?"

"Glad for you."

"Why me?"

"Because you like Henry enough to tackle him on the beach."

"And?"

"I don't," Fonda said. "You should go for him. You know, if you still want to."

Ava H.'s eyes widened. "Seriously? You're stepping down?"

"No." Fonda placed her hand on Ava H.'s shoulder and gave it a sisterly squeeze. "I'm stepping aside." It was a good line. A powerful line. Joan would have been proud.

"And that makes you 'glad'?"

"Very," Fonda said, even though "proud" was more accurate. Her actions finally matched her thoughts, and that took courage. It made her feel grown-up in a way that kissing never would.

Ava H. hugged Fonda so hard they almost toppled onto the sand. "Sorry, I know you don't like being tackled, but thank you!" Giddy from the good news, Ava H. tossed her Lid in the air and returned to her team.

"So, about this dare . . ." Henry said as he hobbled toward Fonda with a slight limp.

Fonda took a step back. "I didn't take it."

"You didn't?"

"No. I picked truth instead." (Her mother would have been proud of that one too.)

Henry shrugged. Without another word, he took off down the beach and returned to the game.

Overwhelmed by a sudden craving for s'mores, Fonda began making her way toward the firepit. She wondered what to do next. Should she tell Drew and Ruthie that she broke their pact? Pretend she went through with it? Say that she tried but Henry turned her down?

Yes, Fonda was a truth picker now. And yes, she wanted her actions to match her thoughts. And they *would*. Her thoughts were saying, *Wait and see what happens with Drew and Ruthie first. Then we'll decide what to tell them.*

And her actions absolutely agreed.

chapter twenty.

DREW SPOTTED WILL by the snack table with Dune Wolsey, Keelie Foster, Kat Evans, and a few other shadowy figures she couldn't identify.

He was biting into a cupcake with a movie star's squint as he gazed out at the ocean, his blond hair silver in the moonlight. It was intoxicating. It was infuriating. It also smelled like onions because Drew was lurking by the trash cans like a hungry raccoon, waiting to make her move.

But what exactly was her move? She thought Will's tongue was gross, and yet, she was admiring him. She had been avoiding him and *still* went looking for him. She wanted to kiss him; she wanted to diss him. The

First-Kiss Club had messed with her internal guidance system. The rules, the pressure, the obligation . . . Drew no longer knew which way was up, where she wanted to go, or how to get there.

She considered asking the universe for guidance. A message in a bottle . . . a whisper in the wind . . . a wise sand crab with a British accent . . . Anything to help cut through this kelp bed of confusion. But Drew already asked for rain and got a starry night, so why bother?

And then . . .

Will's denim-blue high beams spotted Drew. Her inner raccoon froze like a deer. Was he going to run over and greet her? Wave, and ask her to join him? Suggest they go for a moonlit stroll? And if so, what would she say? What did she *want* to say?

Not that it mattered. Will glanced back down at his cupcake and continued his conversation with Dune.

Like.

Drew.

Didn't.

Even.

Exist.

What was happening? Drew was supposed to be the avoider. Not Will. Her internal GPS tried to recalibrate.

Maybe he didn't see her. Maybe his cupcake was about to fall and he had to save it. Maybe Dune said, "Will, look at me while I'm talking to you!" and he did.

Either way, Drew needed answers. If Will was going to ignore her, let him say it to her face.

"Hey!" she said as she approached the picnic table.

"Hey," everyone answered.

Everyone except Will. He was busy pulling the baking cup off a brownie.

"How's it going, *Will*?"

"Good." He jammed the brownie into his mouth. "Howzernigohn?"

"Huh?"

"I said"—he swallowed—"how's your night going?"

How's my night going? Really? That question was for waiters and strangers in elevators. Not the girl you skate with! Not the girl you kissed! Not the girl wearing your necklace! Not that Drew was supposed to care. And yet, she did. "My night is going well, thank you. Yours?"

Will gave her a thumbs-up and a wobbly smile. "Yours?"

"Still going well, thanks."

"Cool."

"Awkward!" Keelie coughed.

Her friends laughed, but Will did not. He just stood there, eyebrows raised, gaze fixed, as if expecting Drew to answer a question he never asked. His warmth had cooled. His spirit had simmered. His volume was down.

Suddenly, Drew's big decision—whether to kiss Will or diss him—no longer felt like hers to make. It seemed like Will's decision now, like he'd already made it. But why?

Sensing the tension, Keelie and her friends began backing away. Drew giggled nervously. Not because any part of this was funny. She just couldn't find the words, so she chose a sound.

"Heads up!" Henry leapt toward them and caught a Frisbee before it hit Drew.

Ava H. appeared and tried to wrest it from his hands. When she couldn't, she jumped on Henry, piggyback style, and rode him back to the shore, shrieking with laughter.

Ava H. and Henry? Where's Fonda? Is she okay?

Suddenly, all thoughts of the FKC vanished. Drew didn't care about bracelets or mints, bathing caps or reunions when she was ninety years old. Those were just things—things that got in the way of her relationships. The nesties didn't need a club to strengthen their bond. It was already strong. But Will? He was more than a crush. More than a first kiss. He was a friend. A friend who was acting like a stranger.

Drew picked up a piece of driftwood and tossed it into the darkness. Yes, things were a bit *bumpy* now, but talking had never been their problem. And Drew didn't want it to be. Not now, not ever. "Want to build a sand-castle?"

"Um . . . not really. It's kind of impossible to see."

"Want to make s'mores?"

Will made a barfy face. "Too much sugar."

"How about we race to the rocks and back?" she asked. "If I win, you have to eat a handful of Atomic Sours, and if you win—"

"They're gone," he said.

"What's gone?"

"The Atomic Sours. I threw them out."

Drew's stomach lurched. He may as well have thrown her out too. "Why didn't you tell me?"

"I went to the dentist yesterday and had a cavity, so I threw them out. It's not a big deal." He started drawing half circles with his toe in the sand.

"Will, is something wrong?" Then, wait. *The dentist!* Had they also fixed Will's tongue fungus—or toungus, as her mom would call it. Had his rocky road been paved?

There was only one way to find out. Before he could answer, Drew said, "I'm glad we're hanging out."

Instead of agreeing, Will scratched the back of his head and muttered, "You don't have to wear that necklace, you know."

Drew's breath hitched. *What's happening?* "I know I don't *have* to wear it. I want to."

"Yeah, well, I kind of got it on a family trip to Hawaii, so . . ."

"So . . . you want it *back*?"

Will looked down at the sand. "Yeah, probably."

Eyes pooling with tears, Drew's hands shook as she struggled to undo the clasp. She felt nauseous. Dizzy.

Like she was drowning from the inside out. She wanted to ask him why this was happening, what she did, how she could undo it. But in the moment, Drew cared less about the past and more about their future. Could they still watch movies in his garage? Could they still talk on the phone? Could they still skate? Funny how she only knew him for a few months and suddenly she couldn't imagine life without him.

Hands still shaking, Drew gave him the necklace. "So now what?"

"I'm going to jump in the ocean."

Before Drew could offer to join, Will walked away. He didn't wave. He didn't look back. He didn't give her one last kiss goodbye. And for the first time that night, Drew really wanted that kiss—bumpy tongue and all.

chapter twenty-one.

RUTHIE FOUND HER TAG friends sitting on blankets by the bonfire, listening to fraternal twins Jayda and Jayden play "Riptide" on their guitars.

"The music drowns out the crying babies," Tomoyo explained.

What about crying souls? Ruthie wanted to say as she scanned the guitar circle for Owen. He wasn't there.

Sage made space for Ruthie on her blanket. "Listen to what they're playing."

"Nice," Ruthie said as she sat.

"*Nice?*" Sage whipped off her black glasses for effect. "It's not *nice*. It's kismet. We *just* said it was our favorite ukulele song this morning, and now they're playing it."

"Oh yeah," Ruthie said, trying her best to sound enthusiastic.

"What's wrong?" Sage asked. "Is it not your favorite anymore?"

"It is. It's just that they're playing it on the guitar, not the ukulele, so . . ." The wind shifted direction, sending smoke from the bonfire straight into Ruthie's eyes. She squinted and turned away.

"Yeah, something is definitely wrong," Sage pressed. "You won't even look at me."

"It's not you, it's the—"

"It's Owen, isn't it?" Sage said. "I mean, where is he?"

Zandra, who was sitting beside them, leaned in. "Do you think he's with Mall Girl?"

Ruthie's jaw clenched. "Maybe." The thought of Owen canoodling with *her* made Ruthie's insides feel like a rickety dam, struggling to hold back a surge of emotions.

Zandra pouted. "And now he's abandoning you and Atom. You must feel terrible." She pulled Ruthie in for a hug and rubbed comforting circles on her back.

"Don't worry," Sage said. "We'll get through this. You may be caught in a riptide now, but—*Lady, running down to the riptide . . .*" she sang, along with everyone else.

"Are you guys talking about Owen?" Everest called over the music.

Sage nodded as she sang.

"He's not Titan material," Tomoyo said. "I knew it the moment I saw his brain board. Brooks Brothers suits *and* Snuggies? Pick a lane, dude."

"Yeah," Sage said. "Like, are you a Ruthie guy or a Mall Girl guy?"

"It's one thing for him to cheat," Everest said. "But quite another for him to walk out on his kid. I would never do that."

"Neither would I," Conrad said.

"Same," Quinn echoed.

The smoke had changed direction, but Ruthie looked away as if it hadn't. She gazed at the ocean, hoping a wave might lift her up and take her back to three weeks ago, before she told Owen she wanted to be just friends, before she became a first-kiss denier or a person who could sit on a beach and allow people to accuse Owen of being a player. Not only was he innocent, he also had no clue he was in the game.

"Ruthie needs to move on," Sage announced. "Am I right?"

Everyone, even the non-TAG kids, began applauding.

Ruthie bristled. "Does the entire school know about this?" she snapped, only to realize they were clapping for Jayda and Jayden, who had finished their song. Still. She couldn't *decide* to like someone new. It didn't work that way.

"See?" Sage said. "You're too wound up. You need a distraction. Someone to make you feel better about yourself."

"Um, I take issue with that," Alberta said. "No one can make Ruthie feel better about herself. Only Ruthie can do that."

Sage rolled her eyes. "I said she needs a *distraction*, Alberta, not a therapy session. Just some new guy to talk to so she forgets about being dumped for a while."

"Thanks for the reminder," Ruthie groaned. But maybe Sage was right. Owen, Atom, the First-Kiss Club, Mall Girl . . . it was all too much. Lighthearted beach banter with someone new might be exactly what she needed. Then, "Okay. I'll try it. But who?"

"Let's rule out TAG'ers. We aren't rebound material, we're long-term relationships only." She pointed at the other side of the firepit. "But what about Tanner Murray? Advanced math, got his braces removed last month, and loves mountain biking."

Ruthie sighed. She liked bikes, but not the mountain kind. Riding on the back of Owen's e-bike was more her speed. "Yeah, I don't know . . ."

"Good. That was a test. Never settle," Sage said. "What about Jake Bly? Plays water polo, got third in last year's spelling bee, and his father owns a Chipotle."

Ruthie squinted through the billowing smoke to find Jake gnawing on his thumbnail with squirrel-like determination. She pointed at the boy beside Jake. "What about him?" He was lying in the sand, arms folded behind his head, gazing up at the stars.

"That's Heaton Hampton," Sage said. "Butter-blond hair, sapphire-blue eyes, athletic but not a jock, solid grades, but no advanced courses. Clearly doesn't own a blanket."

"He seems . . . pensive. I like that."

"There's just one thing," Sage said. "Last year, Steppy told me his armpits smelled like blue cheese. I'm sure he's taken care of it, but just in case . . ." She paused to hear the next song. It was "California Dreamin'." She rolled her eyes. "Let's get you downwind so you can take a whiff of his pits."

"Seriously?" Ruthie laughed. It had been a while since she'd done that.

"They're wide open, so it shouldn't be a problem."

Giggling, they duck-duck-goosed around the circle and stopped a few bodies short of Heaton.

"Stand by for wind gauge." Sage licked her finger and lifted it to the sky. "It's offshore," she said as she drew an X in the sand six feet away from Heaton's left armpit. "Okay, get down."

Cracking up at the absurdity of their mission, Ruthie

held Atom against her chest and did what she was told. Then she cracked up some more.

"Now breathe!" Sage whispered. "Breeeeeeathe."

Ruthie took a sharp inhale. Nothing but smoke and sea air. "No blue cheese!" she whispered to Sage, who was standing above her like a bodyguard.

"Careful! Atom's neck isn't supported."

A *whoosh* of heat spread through Ruthie's body. *Owen?*

"How dare you waltz in at the eleventh hour and criticize Ruthie like that!" Sage shouted above the singing. "Where were you when Atom was crying? Oh, wait, I know. You were with Mall Girl, that's where."

Owen drew back his head. "Mall Girl?"

Ruthie stood. "Sage, don't—"

"Most people would have cracked under the pressure, but not Ruthie. She handled everything. All. By. Her. *Self.*"

"Why are you so mad at me?" he asked. "What did I—"

"How dare you play dumb-dumb with me, Owen Lowell-Klein. You know exactly what you did."

Owen looked to Ruthie and mouthed, "I don't."

Ruthie lowered her gaze.

"If you weren't happy, you should have done the decent thing and dumped her. But cheating? That's undignified."

"*Cheating?*" Owen screeched. "The only time I ever cheated was when I dropped my mini-golf score from 108 to 94. It was my cousin's birthday party, he's incredibly competitive, and I was seven."

"It's okay, Sage," Ruthie said, attempting to stop her. But Sage didn't stop. The music did. And suddenly everyone was watching them.

"Cut the innocent act, Owen," Sage said. "And just so you know, Ruthie has moved on. She likes Heaton Hampton now."

"*Me?!*" Heaton said, pushing himself up onto his elbows. "Who's Ruthie?"

"You like *that* guy?" Owen asked.

"What's wrong with me?"

"Nothing, dude, sorry." Owen took a long, cleansing breath and softened his voice. "Ruthie, I'm sorry I left you with Atom. I would have called, but you don't have a cell phone. And even if you did, it wouldn't have mattered. They're forbidden in the emergency ward."

The heat from Ruthie's *whoosh* cooled. "You were in the emergency ward?"

He nodded. "Franklin got attacked by a Pomapoo at the dog spa and suffered major lacerations. Eleanor saw the whole thing and was traumatized."

Ruthie pouted. "Oh no. Will they be okay?"

Owen nodded again; he was too choked up to speak. This made Ruthie choke up too. She loved his dogs.

"I'm so sorry."

He smiled weakly. "It's not your fault."

"Yeah, well, everything else is." Unable to meet Owen's tear-filled eyes, Ruthie looked away, only to find Fonda and Drew walking toward her. Each of them was coming from a different direction. Both of them were alone.

"How is everything your fault?" Owen asked.

"Everyone thinks we're a thing, and that's why they're mad at you."

"A thing? As in a thing-thing?"

Ruthie nodded.

"You and I?"

Ruthie nodded again.

"Because of Atom?"

A crowd was starting to form, and the waves seemed to quiet. Ruthie wanted to pull Owen aside and continue their conversation in private. And yet, she felt morally obligated to stay where she was and clear his name. She owed him that much.

"Not because of Atom," Ruthie said. "Because I let them think we were."

Owen crinkled his nose. "Why did you want everyone to think we were a thing?"

"So I could—" She caught sight of Fonda and Drew. They had forced their way to the front of the crowd and seemed just as confused as Owen. Ruthie quickly looked away and blurted, "So-I-could-join-a-club."

"A *club*? Why? You already have so many extra-curriculars," Owen said. "What kind of club?"

Fonda and Drew slowly shook their heads.

"A, uh, couple's club," Ruthie said. "For couples. And I wanted you to join. With me."

"That doesn't make any sense," Owen said. "If you wanted to be a *thing*, why did you tell me you wanted to be just friends?"

Ruthie's cheeks began to burn. "I said that?"

"Yes. Last Friday. Right after we . . ." Owen surveyed the audience and shyly said, "You know."

"No," Ruthie said, even though she absolutely did. But did Owen have to talk about it? Right there? In front of everyone?

In.

Front.

Of.

Fonda.

And.

Drew?

"You seriously don't remember?" Owen pressed.

Ruthie shook her head.

"After we . . ." Owen puckered his lips and made kissy sounds. As if no one knew what *that* meant. "You said you wanted me to be your boy *friend*, not your boyfriend. And I agreed. *We agreed.*"

"Wait," Fonda said, stepping closer. "You *already* kissed?"

"Last *Friday*?" Drew said.

"Maybe it was two weekends ago," Owen said. "I'm not sure. My internal clock is off, thanks to Atom . . ."

Ruthie could feel hot anger beams shooting from the nesties' eyes. They penetrated her cheeks, her arms, her skull, her heart.

But Ruthie was angry too. Angry at Owen for outing their kiss. At Drew for talking about kisses in the first place. At Fonda for creating the FKC. At Sage for spreading rumors. But mostly, Ruthie was angry at herself. When would she get over her babyish fear of being left out? If she had told her friends that she had already kissed Owen, that the kiss caught her off guard, and that the club was making her feel pressured, everything would have been fine. She could have helped them research techniques or improved their oral hygiene protocols. There were dozens of ways for Ruthie to stay involved *and* stay true to herself. She had ignored them all.

"This is why everyone is mad at me, isn't it?" Owen

continued. "They think we're a thing and that I cheated on you?"

Ruthie nodded.

Owen scoffed. "With whom?"

"Mall Girl!" Sage said.

"Who's Mall Girl?"

"Dumb-dumb," Sage coughed.

"How am I the dumb one?" Owen pleaded. "Ruthie let everyone think I was a philanderer."

"What's a philanderer?" Heaton asked.

"Dumb-dumb," Sage coughed again.

Atom began to cry.

"Well, you lied to me too!" Ruthie shouted.

"Me?" Owen shrieked. "How? When?"

"I asked who you went to the mall with, and you said no one."

"How is that a *lie*?"

"Because—" Ruthie stopped. Fonda and Drew were just standing there, arms crossed, anger beams blasting, not saying a word.

She couldn't do this anymore, not with everyone

watching. She had cleared Owen's name and ruined her own. The show was over. *She* was over. She wanted to go home. She wanted Foxy.

"Will someone please call my dad and tell him I'm ready to get picked up?"

"You can't just walk away from this, Ruthie," Owen insisted.

And he was right. So she ran.

chapter twenty-two.

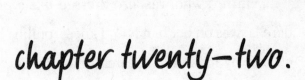

FONDA WOKE TO the thumping beats of Winfrey and Amelia's trap flow remix.

Instead of burying her head under a stack of pillows, she put on her activist outfit: forest-green shirtdress, tan vegan-suede vest, and leopard high-tops. It was Sunday, but Fonda was all business.

The house smelled like onion-dip burps. Refried beans were smeared along the floors, socks hung from the ceiling fan, couch pillows had been jammed in the bathroom. Every surface that hadn't been covered in soda cans revealed a sticky sheen. And, um, were those butt-cheek prints on the flat-screen?

"Nice of you to finally show up," Amelia said as she

raced by with a mop. She was wearing loose sweatpants, an oversized T-shirt, and scrunchie socks. Cleaning had broken her.

Winfrey, who was also dressed like a pre-ball Cinderella, was on her hands and knees, pulling the vacuum cleaner by its cord, in search of an outlet. "Trash bags are in the kitchen," she told Fonda. "Start in the backyard."

Fonda hurried for the front door.

"I said the *back*!" Winfrey called.

"Sorry, but I have my own mess to clean up."

Fonda couldn't help feeling partly responsible for Ruthie's . . . whatever that was last night. If Fonda hadn't started the First-Kiss Club, Ruthie wouldn't have had to hide the fact that she kissed Owen. She wouldn't have had to pretend they were a *thing*, and she wouldn't have spent a week lying to her nesties. Not that Fonda was *totally* okay with Ruthie's secrecy. It hurt knowing that she didn't trust Fonda enough to tell her the truth, that she found out when everyone else did. But she'd be lying to herself if she didn't admit she understood. After all, Fonda wasn't exactly open and honest either. She never told the girls she didn't want to kiss Henry. She didn't give anyone room, herself included, to move at their own pace. And the worst part? Ruthie kissed Owen, and Fonda didn't have any of the juicy details.

✻

As planned, Fonda scooped up Drew on their way to Ruthie's.

"You're dressed up for a Sunday," Drew said.

"So are you."

"Am not. I'm wearing white sweats."

"Yeah, but they're clean."

"Valid point." Drew smiled.

Fonda smiled too, mostly with relief. Drew still hadn't asked about her kiss with Henry and had yet to share details of her kiss with Will. Maybe she had been consumed by the Ruthie scandal and figured their stories could wait. Which was a blessing. Fonda was in no hurry to tell them she changed her mind at the last minute. Breaking a pact was one thing. Breaking a pact she herself had created was quite another.

"Ruthie's still sleeping," Dr. Fran said when she

answered the door. She had her contacts out and her glasses on. This meant she wasn't on call and was probably baking. "I'm concerned. She's usually up by now. Did something happen at the party last night?"

Fonda and Drew exchanged a look.

"Um, she's probably just tired from parenting all week," Fonda said.

"Definitely," Drew said. "We'll check on her, though."

"Wait!" Dr. Fran hurried to the kitchen and returned with a plate of warm blueberry muffins. "Take these. They're her favorite."

Fonda and Drew found Ruthie sitting in bed, legs bent, with Foxy perched on her knees. She was talking to her stuffie. Things were bad.

"Who wants muf-*finns*?" Drew said.

Ruthie quickly lowered her legs and shoved Foxy under the covers. Then she dried her wet cheeks and managed to grin. "Tell me everything, don't leave one thing out," she said, blue eyes red-rimmed and vacant. "How were your kisses?"

"We're not here to talk about *our* kisses. We want to know what happened with yours," Fonda said in her kindest voice. Ruthie didn't need a lecture; she needed an understanding friend. And no one understood how stressful this pact had been more than Fonda.

"It was kind of an accident," Ruthie said. "I told Owen I like having him as a boy friend. He thought I meant boyfriend, and he kissed me."

The girls squealed.

"For, like, a second. And don't ask me to describe it, because I was too shocked to remember. Anyway, we agreed that it was a misunderstanding, and . . . I'm so sorry, you guys," Ruthie said as a fresh set of tears rolled down her cheeks. "I should have told you the truth about Owen. I just wanted to be in the club so badly."

The girls lay down beside her.

"It's my fault," Fonda said. "I never should have started that pact in the first place."

"No, I'm sorry," Drew said. "I never should have obsessed over kissing Will."

She didn't sound the least bit upset that Ruthie broke their pact. And if Drew wasn't upset with Ruthie, maybe she wouldn't be upset with Fonda either.

"You like-liked him for months," Ruthie said. "Of

course you wanted to kiss him. Anyway, it's my fault for letting everyone think Owen and I were a thing."

"Why did you, though?" Drew asked. "I mean, if you weren't into him, why didn't you pick another guy? Or just tell us you weren't into anyone? We would have understood."

Fonda tensed. Pretending to like a boy, just to fit in, was her crime too. And it sounded even more pathetic when spoken out loud.

"That's the thing," Ruthie said. "It turns out I do like Owen."

"That's great!" Drew said.

"No, it's not. He likes Mall Girl."

"Still," Fonda said. "At least you know you like Owen for Owen, and not some kiss pact."

"That's what Foxy said," Ruthie told them. "But whatever, it doesn't make me feel better." She shook her head, as if trying to erase the current conversation and make room for a new one. "Anyway, I want to talk about you guys. Fonda, did you kiss Henry?"

"Yes," Fonda said.

"You did?" Drew screeched.

"Yup. I kissed him goodbye. Minus the actual kiss part."

Drew cocked her head. "Huh?"

"Ava H. really likes him, and—"

"And?"

"And . . ." Fonda paused. Her sisters had been right all along: she was an immature, puberty-challenged girl, doomed to a braless, boy-less existence. But this was Drew and Ruthie, not Winfrey and Amelia. The nesties did sisterhood right. So, after a gusty exhale, Fonda looked at them and said, "I wasn't ready."

Drew gave her a fabric-softener-scented hug and said, "At least Henry *would* have kissed you if you wanted him to. I tried to kiss Will, and he ran away."

Fonda hugged Drew back. "It's okay. You can be honest with us. I just admitted I wasn't ready. You can too."

"I am being honest," she insisted. "He asked for his necklace back. He hates me, and I don't know why."

"Maybe Will's not ready either," Fonda said, feeling like a different kind of kissing expert. The kind who knows how *not* to do it.

"But he *is* ready," Drew said.

"How do you know?" Ruthie asked.

"Well . . ." Drew faltered. "Last Wednesday, he sort of—"

"Oh my DOG!" Ruthie said. "You too?!"

Drew nodded.

Fonda crossed her arms. Was she hurt all over again? Yes. Yes, she was. Drew and Ruthie *both* kissed and didn't tell.

And.

They.

Were.

Supposed.

To.

Tell.

Each.

Other.

EVERYTHING.

"Let me guess," she managed. "You didn't tell us because of the pact."

Drew nodded. "And I didn't want you to think I was some kind of kissing maniac who couldn't control herself."

"Too late," Fonda teased. "So how was it?"

"Bumpy," Drew said.

"Bumpy?" Ruthie giggled. "Were you on a skate-board?"

"No. It was more of a tongue-texture thing."

"Like Bubble Wrap?" Fonda asked.

"More like sandpaper."

"Ew!" they squealed.

"I'm not a doctor, but I don't think that's normal," Ruthie said as she reached for a muffin. "Let's ask my mom."

Drew swatted the muffin from Ruthie's hand. "No way! This is private."

"What did you say?" Fonda asked, grateful that she didn't kiss Henry. What if he had a bumpy tongue too?

"I didn't say anything. I avoided him for the rest of the week."

"He probably thinks you stopped liking him," Ruthie said.

"Did you?" Fonda asked.

"No." Drew began picking her cuticles. "I was just super freaked out. But he went to the dentist on Friday, and I think he got it fixed." She sighed. "Not that I'll ever know."

Fonda gazed at the puzzles on Ruthie's walls. They too had been broken into a thousand pieces. And in time, they'd been put back together. There was hope.

"You should talk to Will. Ask him why he acted like that," Fonda said.

Drew sighed again. "Maybe."

"I would do it soon," Ruthie pressed. "Before he finds his own Mall Girl."

"The truth does feel better," Fonda told them. "Even when it hurts."

Ruthie snickered. "Foxy said that too."

"Drew, you ask Will why he asked for his necklace back, and Ruthie, you tell Owen you like-like him."

"Yeah, no," Ruthie said. "I already tried to tell Owen, and it didn't go so well."

"What happened?"

"I ran home."

"Why?" Drew asked.

"Mall Girl was there."

Fonda rolled her eyes. "So, he doesn't know."

"No."

"Ruthie, when Owen tried to kiss you, you shut him down. And, Drew, when Will kissed you, you avoided him for the rest of the week. Is that right?"

They nodded.

"Um, are you seeing a pattern here? You made them think you didn't like them."

"I don't know . . ." Ruthie's voice trailed off.

"Will was pretty clear about how he felt last night." Drew pouted.

"Whatever. You need answers," Fonda said. "I'll be here for you no matter what they are. Hey, I know. Let's make an 'I'm here for you' pact!"

Two blueberry muffins hit Fonda in the forehead. Laughing, she devoured them both. It was the first decent meal she'd had all week.

chapter twenty-three.

RUTHIE APPROACHED OWEN'S door with a poster board in her hand and Atom strapped to her back, ready but not ready for what was about to happen.

As she reached for the doorbell, a gray cumulus cloud drifted in front of the sun. Was this a sign? Was Ruthie's romantic forecast calling for rain? Was the rest of her life destined to be gray? As Fonda said earlier, there was only one way to find out.

Seconds later, Owen opened the door. Were his parents *ever* home?

"Hey!" he said, tightening his black bathrobe. "What are you doing here?" He sounded excited. *Too* excited.

And quickly flattened his tone. "I don't get Atom until three. Was there a change in the schedule?"

"Uh, n-no," Ruthie stammered. "I just wanted to show you this hack I figured out." She unclipped her harness and removed Atom. "I put duct tape on his speaker. It muffles his cries. I slept like a baby last night. Which, technically, is a weird thing to say, since babies are the worst sleepers ever."

Owen reached for the back of his neck. "I don't get it."

"It's simple," Ruthie explained. "Duct tape is made with pressure-sensitive adhesive that—"

"I understand how duct tape works, Ruthie. I don't get why you're here. Last night you called me a liar, publicly accused me of cavorting with some Mall Girl, and then ran off. And now you're acting all normal and Ruthie-ish?"

Owen was right. She was *acting*—acting like nothing had happened.

"Is that why you're here?" Owen asked. "To talk about duct tape?"

Ruthie returned Atom to his harness. "Actually, I,

uh, I came to check up on Franklin and Eleanor. Are they okay?"

"Thank you for asking," he said politely. "They'll be home tomorrow."

"Phew," Ruthie said as she struggled to find the right words.

In school, the more she studied, the better she did. But outside the classroom, she could still be an epic failure, no matter how hard she tried. So how exactly was TAG preparing her for real life? "Owen, can I ask you something?"

He nodded.

"Why did you say you went to the mall alone the other day? Why did you lie?"

"I didn't *lie*."

"But I saw you with that girl."

He ran his hand across his Lego-figurine hair as if coaxing his brain to remember. "You mean *Meg*?"

"Sure, if that's what you want to call her," Ruthie said. "You could have told me you were into her. You didn't have to—"

"Into her?" He cut a look to the poster board Ruthie

was hiding behind her back. The one she spent an hour making after her pep talk from the nesties. The one she would probably never have the courage to show him. "Meg's my friend. Our moms are in the same romance book club, but we didn't go to the mall together. We ran into each other by coincidence. She was picking up a book for her mom, and I was picking up a book for mine. Ever since we got e-bikes, they've been sending us on all kinds of errands. It's super annoying."

"But . . . then why was she at your house?" Ruthie asked, not yet able to use Mall Girl's real name.

"The moms always put us together during their meetings. The other kids were on the way. Meg just got here first."

"Oh." Ruthie's swirling thoughts settled, and her heartbeat slowed. Another misunderstanding. And this one was on her. "I'm really sorry."

"For what?" Owen asked. "Thinking I'm a liar, or telling everyone I'm a cheater?"

"Both."

Owen stuffed his hands in the pockets of his robe and rocked back on his heels. "It's okay. I forgive you."

"You do?"

"Yeah. Everyone thought I was a ladies' man. That might never happen again."

"But you are!" Ruthie said. "Mall—I mean, Meg— likes you. I could tell by the way she looked at me when I came to the door."

"Yeah, well, she's not my semicolon. You are."

Ruthie felt a sting of adrenaline. "Wait, what did you say?" Did Owen seriously just use her semicolon analogy? But how?

"I heard you practicing on my security cam," he said shyly. "Saying that you want to be apart but together, like a—"

"So were you just saying that to mess with me, or did you mean it?"

"I meant it," he said. Then he raised his eyebrows. "Did you?"

Ruthie gave him the poster.

"Is this a brain board?"

She nodded.

"Rhea asked you to make one?"

"No."

"Then why did you?"

"To show you what's been on my mind."

Owen took in the picture of Ruthie, the picture of himself, and the semicolon in between. He lifted his gaze with a smile that reached all the way up to his eyes. It was so warm, so bright, it made her forget all about that gray cumulus. "You think about . . . *me*?"

Cheeks burning, Ruthie nodded.

"Wanna start over?" Owen asked, still beaming.

Ruthie nodded again.

Owen offered his right hand.

Ruthie took it.

Then they shook.

And shook.

And shook.

Owen holding Ruthie's hand; Ruthie holding Owen's.

Apart, but together.

Just like a semicolon.

chapter twenty-four.

DREW LANDED ANOTHER ollie. Her fifth in a row. When she made it to ten, she'd call Will. If she messed up, she'd start over, and the call would have to wait. It was a flawed strategy in that Drew wanted to make ten ollies in a row. Who wouldn't? But the reward was more of a punishment. Not that Drew didn't want to talk to Will. She did! It was the possibility of another rejection that made her want to barf in her helmet.

As she landed number six, Drew thought of the last time she and Will had fun together. It was right there on her front lawn, just before they kissed. Looking at the spot made her want to barf in her helmet a second time.

Not because of the tongues, not anymore. But because of her tragic timing—Drew was over the bumps, but now Will was over Drew.

But what if he wasn't?

Ollie number seven.

Ollie number eight.

Ollie number nine.

Ollie number ten.

Dang! It was an all-time high wrapped in an all-time low.

Drew kicked her board into her hand and sat on the curb. The setting sun created one long shadow behind her. She thought of Will. How it should have been two.

She took out her phone.

What would she say? What would he say? What if he didn't answer? What if he did?

Drew put the phone away.

She promised Fonda and Ruthie she'd call Will before sundown.

Drew took out her phone again. She tapped Will's number.

It rang.

And rang. And rang.

She ended the call.

Three rings were more than enough time to answer. He was avoiding her. Unless he was about to answer and she hung up.

She tapped his number again.

It rang. And rang.

Drew ended the call and got back on her board.

She skated.

Stopped.

Tapped.

Panicked.

Ended.

Skated.

Stopped.

Tapped.

Panicked.

Ended.

What was *wrong* with her? Why was this so hard? She put the phone in her pocket, hopped onto her board again, and skated as fast as she could.

And skated.

And skated.

Picking up speed.

Up one street.

Down another.

Drew wanted to skate until the energy stopped surging and her thoughts stopped Willing. She didn't want to think about their effortless conversations, the things they had in common, his denim-blue eyes, her vibrating back pocket . . .

She stopped. It was her phone. Someone was calling her. Hands shaking, Drew checked the screen and—

Will!

She kicked up her board and dared herself to answer.

"Hello?" she said, trying not to sound out of breath.

"Hey. Did you call, like, fifteen times?"

"No. I'm skating. It must have been a butt dial."

"Wow, how badly does your butt want to talk to me?"

"I don't know, you'll have to ask it."

Will laughed. Drew didn't, even though she was tempted to. Laughing might imply that everything was fine. That they could carry on as if nothing had happened and skip over the uncomfortable conversation. But Drew had done enough avoiding. Not only was it weak; it was also pointless. Avoidance didn't erase problems; it made them bigger.

"But while I have you," she began, "I just wanted to say that I'm sorry we didn't hang out Thursday or Friday. I had a bad headache. It hurt to talk."

White lies don't count as avoidance, do they?

"Okay."

"Okay?"

"Yeah, it's okay," Will said. No questions. No doubts. Nothing to add. Either he wanted to end the awkwardness and get back to the good old days, or he just wanted to end the awkwardness and get off the phone.

"So, do you still want to hang out?" Drew pressed.

"Sure."

"Then why were you acting weird last night?"

Will went silent.

"Hello?" she asked. "Are you still there?"

"Yeah," he said softly. "It's just that—" He paused. "I'm sorry I kissed you."

"Uh, okay," Drew said, not quite sure how to take that. "Why?"

Will let out a sharp exhale and said, "You seemed super freaked out after. Like you didn't want to talk to me anymore. It's just, I thought you wanted . . . If I knew you didn't, I never would have—"

"That's not it," Drew told him as relief washed over her.

"It's not?"

"No."

"Then why did you leave so quickly? Why did you stop talking to me at school?"

Drew hesitated. No more lies. "It wasn't a headache. It was a tongue thing. But it's okay! You don't have to be embarrassed. I'm totally fine with it now," she said. "Did you get it fixed?"

"Did *I* get it fixed?" he asked. "What about you?"

"What about me?"

"Did you get yours fixed?"

"My tongue?" Drew said. "Why would I fix my tongue?"

"It was kind of . . . catlike." She could hear him smiling a little bit.

"And yours was gravelly," Drew fired back. "Isn't that why you went to the dentist? To get medicine or something?"

"No. I had a cavity."

"And she didn't say anything about your tongue?"

"*He,*" Will corrected. "And no, he didn't. Because my tongue is fine. You're the one who needs medicine."

"I am not!" Drew said, laughing. "And I can prove it."

"Really? How?" Will asked. Then, "Hold on, someone just rang my bell."

Moments later, Will opened his front door and beamed.

"Stick out your tongue," Drew told him.

Will stuck out his tongue.

Slipping into nurse mode, she shined her phone's flashlight on his lingua and inspected it. "Hmm . . . no unusual ridges. No fungus-y growths. No discoloration." She lowered her phone. "All good under the hood."

Will stepped closer. "Your turn." He smelled like coconut-scented sunscreen.

Drew stuck out her tongue confidently and said, "Ahhhh."

"Yeah." Will's eye was practically in Drew's mouth. "It checks out."

"Told you!"

"Told *you!*"

They stood there looking at each other until he broke the silence. "So you didn't avoid me because I kissed you?"

"No," Drew said. "I wanted you to kiss me. I was freaked out about your bumpy tongue."

"Well, I was freaked out about *your* bumpy tongue, and I didn't avoid you."

Drew squared her shoulders. "Wait, are you being serious? I really had a bumpy tongue?"

Will nodded.

"But how?" Drew said, sinking a little. How could she have been so shallow? How lucky was she that he wasn't? "Maybe we should do another kind of inspection," Drew said as her insides stirred. "Just to be sure?"

"Maybe we should."

Drew took a step forward.

Will did the same.

Drew leaned in.

Will leaned in too.

Their lips met. Then their tongues. His was warm, soft, *smooth*.

Drew pulled back. "You're not a driveway!"

Will beamed. "And you're not a cat!"

"Hey, wanna go to Fresh & Fruity tomorrow after school and celebrate?" Drew asked.

"Sure. But no more Atomic Sours. I think they gave me that cavity."

Drew narrowed her eyes and cocked her head. "Wait. Do you think . . . ?"

"Do I think *what*?"

"Do you think the Atomic Sours made our tongues bumpy?"

Will's eyebrows shot up. "Dr. Savo did say that acidic candy ravages tooth enamel. Maybe it ravages tongues too."

"That must be it. When we stopped eating the Atomic Sours, our Atomic Tongues cleared up."

Without warning, Will leaned in, held the side of Drew's face, and kissed her again.

No one knew about it, and no one was watching. It was just for them. Exactly the way a second first kiss should be.

chapter twenty-five.

FONDA LEANED INTO her dinner plate and took a whiff of what looked like a hockey puck. All she smelled was the powder-scented incense and vanilla candles her sisters had been burning to mask the stench of onion-dip-burp smell left behind by their party. She glanced outside the kitchen window at the dark, silent street. Why was her mother taking so long?

"Winfrey, you've outdone yourself," Amelia said, poking at the charred patty.

"You've also outdone the meat," Fonda mumbled. She didn't mention the blue potatoes, which were back on the table. Reheated and repulsive.

"Don't touch!" Winfrey snipped. "Wait for Joan."

Car lights cut through the darkness.

Winfrey bristled. "Mom!"

"Napkins on laps," Amelia said.

"Why are you guys so stressed? She's not going to find out about the party," Fonda said. "The house looks great."

"No thanks to you," Winfrey hissed.

"No offense, but I wasn't even here last night."

"We're a team," Amelia said. "We're supposed to help each other."

"Some team," Fonda scoffed. "You literally uninvited me to the party."

"You were literally asking for it," Winfrey said.

She's right. I did ask for it. But still. A team? Really?

"Yeah, well, I'm glad I did," Fonda said, not apologizing.

"Dude," Amelia said. "Why have you been so aggro lately?"

Fonda considered saying she was tired of being treated like a baby, of being disrespected and mocked. That she was a capable, maturing pre-woman and would like to be treated as such. But that would have made

Fonda sound even more aggro, and she wasn't. She was simply standing up for herself, and her sisters weren't used to it.

Neither was she.

Even though her boobs hadn't grown, her lips hadn't been kissed, and her period hadn't come, something inside Fonda had shifted. It began Friday night when she spoke her mind to Winfrey and Amelia, then continued when she let Henry go and broke the pact. Perhaps instead of relying on others to make her feel seen, Fonda was starting to see herself. And maybe, just maybe, she liked what she saw.

Instead of sharing any of that, Fonda simply said, "I forgive you."

"*You* forgive *us*?" Winfrey practically spat. "What did *we* do?"

Fonda hooked a finger under her friendship bracelets. "It doesn't matter anymore. It's all good. Let's move on."

"Maybe she's not too aggro," Amelia said to Winfrey. "Maybe she's too *chill*."

"Yeah, something is definitely up," Winfrey said. Then to Fonda, "Did Rocket Raccoon propose?"

"Win, what if she likes a boy this time?" Amelia teased. "An actual human?"

"Ahhhh," Winfrey squealed. "Did Fondle kiss a boy?"

"No, but I could have."

"Cold feet?" Winfrey asked.

"Nope."

"Cold sore?" Amelia asked.

"Nope."

"Then why didn't you?"

"I wasn't ready," Fonda said proudly.

She waited for their laughter. Waited for their teasing. Instead, their smug expressions softened and warmth emerged, like rays of sunshine after a storm.

"I wasn't ready until I was fourteen," Amelia said.

"You *are* fourteen," Winfrey said.

"I'm fourteen and a half."

"I was ready on my thirteenth birthday," Winfrey told them. "But everyone is different. You're not ready until you're ready, and you can't rush it. Same goes for wearing makeup, riding a short board, and eating sashimi. When the time is right, you know. You know?"

Fonda nodded, stunned by Winfrey's genuine display of humanity, hungry for more.

But the doorbell rang. Time was up.

"It's Joan!" Winfrey began waving a stick of incense.

"Why would Mom ring the doorbell?" Amelia asked.

"Who cares? Maybe she forgot her keys. Napkins on laps!"

Ignoring them, Fonda hurried to greet her mother.

It wasn't Joan.

It was Ruthie.

"I did it!" she announced as she ran into the house, hands waving wildly. "Ruthie got truthie and—" She stopped short when she noticed Winfrey and Amelia sitting stiffly at the table. "Sorry, am I interrupting something?"

"No, it's cool. They're cool," Fonda said.

Ruthie raised her eyebrows. *Since when?*

"Tell me," Fonda insisted. "What happened?"

"Mall Girl is just a friend! Owen thinks we're semi-colons! And we held hands!"

Winfrey and Amelia gave each other confused looks. The doorbell rang again.

"Joan!" Winfrey said. "OMG, there's a Dorito by the stove! Ruthie, get it!"

"But—"

"Now!" Amelia bellowed.

Fonda hurried to answer the door again; it was Drew.

"The bumpy tongues were from the Atomic Sours!" she yelled, running into the house. She also stopped short, not when she saw Amelia and Winfrey, but when she saw Ruthie. "Are you gonna eat that chip? I'm starving."

Ruthie handed it to her. Drew ate it. Winfrey and Amelia looked at each other, horrified.

"So everything is good between you and Will?"

Drew gave her a thumbs-up. "All smooth, if you know what I mean."

Fonda and Ruthie threw their arms around Drew and bounced for joy.

"Tragic," Winfrey said, rolling her eyes.

"Middle schoolers," Amelia added.

But Fonda kept on laughing. So what if her sisters

thought the nesties were tragic weirdos? They *were* tragic weirdos. It was the best!

Joan coughed as she walked into the kitchen. "What's going on in here? It smells like onions and incense." She set an extra-large pizza box on the counter. Fonda wasn't sure which to embrace first.

"Mom!" Fonda called as she ran toward her.

"Well, *someone's* happy to see—"

Fonda took the pizza box to the table, whipped open the top.

"Oh, Winfrey, I had no idea you were going to cook." Joan pouted. "We could always save the pizza for another—"

"NOOOO!" everyone shouted. Even Winfrey!

"Can Drew and Ruthie stay for dinner?" Fonda asked.

"Of course!" Joan said as they gathered around the table.

Once seated, Fonda leaned toward Joan and whispered, "Thanks for the pizza."

"Thanks for telling me to get it," Joan whispered back. "Are those potatoes blue?"

"Yep."

"And did I see butt-cheek prints on the flat-screen?"

"Yep."

"Should I bother asking?"

Fonda took an enormous bite. "Nope." Grease slithered down her wrist, and warm, gooey pizza filled her soul. Then—

Ouch.

She was blindsided by an unexpected stomach cramp. *Hmmm.* Good times were supposed to fill her belly with warm tingles, not steely claws. Still, she took another bite. Her stomach was probably acclimating to real food.

Another cramp quickly followed.

"Be right back," Fonda announced as she hurried for the bathroom.

Once inside, she locked the door, pulled down her jeans, and—

Was that blood in her underwear?

Was it appendicitis? Irritable bowel syndrome? Leaky gut? Her heart started speeding; her vision coned. She was too young to die.

Unless . . .

She recalled her cramp-filled week, her newfound sense of power.

Could it be?

Fonda looked at her underwear again.

It *was*!

Tears filled her eyes.

Finally!

And to think all the people she wanted to tell were right there in the next room.

✺

When Fonda returned to the kitchen, Drew was showing Winfrey and Amelia how to juggle potatoes, and Ruthie was interviewing Joan about her conference.

"Are you feeling okay?" her mother asked.

"I'm feeling great." Fonda smiled coyly. *"Period."*

"Good," Joan said. Then to play along, she added, "Period."

"I mean, I'm feeling a little different, I guess. Maybe a little older. *Period.*"

"Older?" Joan asked. "How? Question mark."

"Period," Fonda said. "Per-i-od."

Winfrey, who was mid-juggle, allowed the potatoes to fall to the floor. "Did you get your period?"

"Wait, what?" Joan said.

Fonda nodded as tears of joy flooded her eyes.

"Exclamation point!" Drew shouted.

"And I'm a semicolon," Ruthie added.

"I'll get the pads," Amelia offered.

"That's okay," Fonda said. "I have everything I need." She sprang up from the table. "I'll show you."

Fonda ran to her bedroom and pulled her period purse from her backpack. Poor thing had been all dressed up with nowhere to go for months. Now it could finally hit the scene, red-carpet style!

When she returned to the kitchen, Joan was pulling ingredients from the pantry so she could bake a celebratory cake. Winfrey and Amelia offered to teach her how to dress for maximum comfort. And Drew and Ruthie were bombarding her with questions—questions Fonda could finally answer. She had experience now. Not on first kisses, but on first periods.

And the timing couldn't have been more perfect.

Acknowledgments

Hi! Thought you could get rid of me, didn't you? Nope, I'm still here. If I'm being honest, I feel a little sad. I truly love these characters, and I miss them already. They are kind people with noble intentions who mess up all the time. We all do. (See my dedication for proof.)

Over the years, I've come to realize that it's not about the mistakes you make, but rather what you do after you make them. Have you owned your part? Did you learn anything? Are you going to do better next time? Have you forgiven yourself? If you answered yes, then you, my friend, are doing wrong right. That's all humans can hope for. If I did everything perfectly, I certainly wouldn't have needed the following people to help me complete this novel. And believe me, I needed every one of them.

I needed Jennifer Klonsky, president and publisher at Putnam, to demand the best from me, and assistant editor Matt Phipps to keep things moving along.

I needed Josh Bank, Sara Shandler Banks, and Lanie Davis to help me shape this story. (Lanie, you are a brilliant editor. Thank you!)

I needed Dina Santorelli for her wildly appreciated assistance and Emmy Regal for keeping the story bible updated.

I needed my agent, Richard Abate, who made me laugh when I was overwhelmed, and Martha Stevens, my don.

I needed Jessica Jenkins and Judit Mallol to design this cover. Nicole Rheingans to make the inside pages fabulous. And I really, really, really needed copy editors Ariela Rudy Zaltzman, Diane João, and Cindy Howle.

Mom and Best Sis, I know you're the only ones in my family reading this. So you're the only ones getting thanked. If any of my deadbeat relatives or offspring *happen* upon this page, speak up, and I'll name my next novel *I Underestimated You Stuff*. But something tells me that won't happen.

Mostly, I needed you, the reader. You have given the tween voices in my head a reason to live.

Thank you.

Xoxo Lisi

THERE'S ALWAYS MORE GIRL STUFF!

Turn the page for a peek at the first two books in the series!

Fonda, Drew, and Ruthie have been besties forever, but there's nothing like seventh grade to test the bonds of friendship. Can they survive the challenges of crushes and cliques?

girl stuff.

lisi harrison
#1 BESTSELLING AUTHOR

chapter one.

FONDA MILLER GLUED a picture to her vision board and smiled a little. It was a half-staff smile that, if texted, would require two emojis since it felt happy *and* sad at the same time.

In the picture, she and her best friends, Drew Harden and Ruthie Goldman, were lying in a heap on Fonda's front lawn laughing themselves breathless. It had been taken two months earlier, back in June, moments before five heartless parents ripped them apart.

They had been so upset about saying goodbye for the summer that they tied their ankles together in protest. While they were tying, Fonda's mother, Joan, had tried to convince them the eight weeks would fly by. Then Drew's dad chimed in from the driveway next door.

"The separation will be healthy. Especially since you'll be going to the same school when you get back."

"He's right," said Mrs. Harden. "Nesties need breaks every now and then."

Drew rolled her hazel eyes. Probably because she couldn't stand when her mother combined words. "Why can't she say *neighbors* and *besties* like a normal person?" Drew snorted, which made Ruthie and Fonda laugh harder.

And Ruthie's parents, well, they were at work wrapping things up before their family road trip to Washington, DC. But if the Goldmans had been there, they would have said something like *Poplar Creek is beautiful, but there's no culture here and even less diversity. It's important to leave our sunny Southern California bubble and explore the outside world.* That was the kind of thing they always said. Learning was their cardio.

The parents were only trying to help. But their words couldn't fill the pit of loneliness inside Fonda's stomach. They couldn't make long summer days fly by. And they couldn't bike to town for frozen yogurt. They were nothing more than verbal Band-Aids, well-intended distractions that never fully stuck.

So, with their ankles bound together by a worn skipping rope, Fonda, Drew, and Ruthie took big stubborn strides toward the top of their cul-de-sac. *Goodbye, Poplar Creek, and hello, someplace where grown-ups let "nesties" spend summers together. Someplace with free fro-yo and unlimited toppings!*

Then . . . *Thunk.*

Within seconds, they fell out of step with one another and timbered onto Fonda's front lawn, and they were separated the next day.

Now, two months later, Fonda couldn't wait to see them again, and she doubly couldn't wait for them to see her new, ultrasophisticated flat-ironed hair. Only three more sleeps . . .

Fonda, Drew, and Ruthie are on a mission to make sure their seventh-grade field trip is the best ever, but everything's getting in their way—including their hearts.

crush stuff.

a *girl stuff* novel

lisi harrison

#1 BESTSELLING AUTHOR

chapter one.

IN THE MOVIES, Halloween season—or what boring people call October—is depicted by howling wind, skeletal tree branches, and creeping shadows. But in Poplar Creek, California, where wind is more of a lazy sigh, palm fronds sway like a fresh blowout, and the sun is too bright for shadows, Halloween season ushers in a different type of terror, one that Fonda Miller named the Seventh-Grade Slopover.

"The Ferdink Farms field trip is pure hell," Fonda said as she, Drew, and Ruthie walked home from Poplar Middle School. It was Friday, and the next-door besties, or nesties, as they called themselves, were spending the night at Fonda's. Her stride should have had spring, her steps pep. But the feet in her leopard-print high-tops were heavy with dread because this year's Seventh-Grade Slopover would be no different than last year's Sixth-Grade Slopover. And no different was no bueno.

"How bad can it be?" Ruthie asked, her wide blue eyes beaming optimism. And who could blame her? The students in the Talented and Gifted program were also invited. Which meant that for three days and two nights, Ruthie and her TAG friends would have the same schedule as Fonda and Drew. It was something Ruthie had always wanted. It was something they had all wanted. But not like this.

"Two nights, three days, and seven meals of nothing but pig slop. That's how bad." Fonda removed the mirrored heart-shaped sunglasses she'd "borrowed" from her sister Amelia so they could see the panic in her eyes. "We shovel horse poo, milk cows, and sleep on mattresses that smell like oily grandfather scalp."

"My grandfather is bald, so his scalp doesn't smell oily," Ruthie said. "His has more of a minty smell. Hey, maybe my mattress will smell minty!"

"Then mine will smell like sticky notes," Drew said, because her Grandpa Lou tacked Post-it reminders all over the house so her Grandma Mae wouldn't forget anything.

"I bet Weird-O's mattress is gonna smell like money," Fonda said, pointing at the boy who lived at the top of their street. He was ambling up his driveway, shoulders rounded and neck arched, as he thumbed the screen of his phone. His rich, preppy, private-school look—button-down shirt, white sneakers, and corn-tortilla-colored slacks—might be on point in Connecticut or, say, Boston—but it completely missed the point in California. Everything about Weird-O missed the point.

"His name is Owen Lowell-Kline," Ruthie said, defending him as usual. Not because she liked Owen, or even really knew him. But because two years earlier, he bought her entire supply of Girl Scout cookies, which freed her up to go to the beach with Fonda and Drew. "I feel bad for him."

"Why?" Drew asked. "Because he ate fifty boxes of Do-si-dos?"

"They weren't *all* Do-si-dos. There were Samoas and Tagalongs too. And, no. I feel bad for Owen because he doesn't have any friends."

"Because he's a pick-me," Fonda said. If Ruthie had ever had the misfortune of being in class with Owen and witnessed him waving his hand at the teacher while shouting, "Pick me, pick me," she would have felt bad for *herself*, not Owen.

"Just because he's a pick-me doesn't mean you have to be a pick-on-him," Ruthie said. Then she laughed. Everyone did. Because it was one of the clunkiest comebacks of all time.